Praise for *Girl*

"A masterpiece, a heart-wrenching story of loss and redemption powerfully rendered in O'Brien's singular voice, which is at once fierce and tender, conscientious and visionary."

—Dawn Miranda Sherratt-Bado, *The Irish Times*

"*Girl* is a superb example what fiction is supposed to be: an act of empathetic imagination . . . *Girl* is Edna O'Brien saying, we must write—and read—about each other, or fiction will die."

—Charles Taylor, *Los Angeles Review of Books*

"*Girl* is [Edna O'Brien's] nineteenth novel and she has intimated that it may be her last. It may yet prove to be her most powerful."

—Sean O'Hagan, *The Guardian*

"Edna O'Brien tells this story with such compassion and understanding that the very disturbing events she relates are uplifting—and unforgettable. An utterly unique achievement." —Ian McKellen

"While the author writes about a culture wholly different from her own, she does so not just with grace and compassion but with Nigerian songs, tales and myths."

—Bethanne Patrick, *The Washington Post*

"This is Auden's Icarus story, though it happens at eye level, right on planet Earth, while everyone's looking—or could. It's horrific, as the writer intended, though the Girl endures and is finally released from many forms of captivity, into the light. It's never wan, the light of love." —Ann Beattie

"O'Brien's portrait of war, powerfully narrated . . . against a rich backdrop of cultural rituals and myths, is downright haunting."

—*People*

"A story of indoctrination and resistance, *Girl* is told in a prose so butter-smooth and sprueless it seems to have fallen fully-formed from O'Brien's pen. The book's sudden outbursts of stomach-turning violence come like speed bumps in the greater purl, made more jolting and haunting still by the terrible, clear-eyed maturity of the writing. It's a sort of tight-rope act O'Brien seems to be performing, strung between the stream-like nature of her prose and the painful shards of her story."
—Bailey Trela, *Ploughshares*

"By an extraordinary act of the imagination we are transported into the inner world of a girl who, after brutal abuse as a slave to Nigerian jihadis, escapes and with dogged persistence begins to rebuild her shattered life. *Girl* is a courageous book about a courageous spirit."
—J. M. Coetzee

"The lauded Irish novelist leaps continents in a feat of imagination that transmogrifies headlines into a searing fable of violence and resilience . . . In spare, exacting prose, O'Brien aims her saga, like a divining rod, at 'the best of all knowing and feeling and forgiving.'"
—O, *The Oprah Magazine*

"Burning with rage and anguish, yet woven from glittering prose, *Girl* is a riveting story of the unbreakable bonds between mothers, daughters, and sisters."
—Angela Ledgerwood and Adrienne Westenfeld, *Esquire*

"A haunting tale of suffering and innocence defiled. Remarkable in its trajectory from darkness through to a hard-won glimmer of light. Fierce and lyrical by turns. Another magnificent book from a magnificent writer."
—Marina Carr

"*Girl* is a novel of profound and ever-renewing empathy and grace—a parable on the complex subject of human redemption. Its verbal funds are clear and transporting and unforgettable; its dramatic resources vast."
—Richard Ford

Murdo MacLeod

A NOTE ABOUT THE AUTHOR

EDNA O'BRIEN has written more than twenty works of fiction, most recently *The Little Red Chairs*. She is the recipient of numerous awards, including the Prix Femina, the PEN/Nabokov Award for Achievement in International Literature, the Irish PEN Lifetime Achievement Award, the National Arts Club Medal of Honor, and the Ulysses Medal. Born and raised in the west of Ireland, she has lived in London for many years.

GIRL

EDNA O'BRIEN

PICADOR

FARRAR, STRAUS AND GIROUX

NEW YORK

Picador
120 Broadway, New York 10271

The Library of Congress has cataloged the Farrar, Straus and Giroux hardcover
edition as follows:

Names: O'Brien, Edna, author.
Title: Girl / Edna O'Brien.
Description: First American edition. | New York : Farrar, Straus and Giroux, [2019]
Identifiers: LCCN 2019020325 | ISBN 9780374162559 (hardcover)
Classification: LCC PR6065.B7 G56 2019 | DDC 823/.914—dc23
LC record available at https://lccn.loc.gov/2019020325

Picador Paperback ISBN: 978-1-250-23991-4

Our books may be purchased in bulk for promotional, educational, or business
use. Please contact your local bookseller or the Macmillan Corporate and
Premium Sales Department at 1-800-221-7945, extension 5442, or by e-mail at
MacmillanSpecialMarkets@macmillan.com.

Picador® is a U.S. registered trademark and is used by Macmillan Publishing
Group, LLC, under license from Pan Books Limited.

For book club information, please visit facebook.com/picadorbookclub or
e-mail marketing@picadorusa.com.

picadorusa.com • instagram.com/picador
twitter.com/picadorusa • facebook.com/picadorusa

1 3 5 7 9 10 8 6 4 2

For the Mothers and Daughters
of
North East Nigeria

We have helicopters now that can fire four thousand rounds per minute. A truly devastating piece of military hardware. A game changer.

Nigerian government statement
in response to Boko Haram

'Here's linen to clothe your wounds.'

Hecuba to the defiled daughters of Troy.
Euripides, *The Trojan Women*

I WAS A GIRL ONCE, but not any more. I smell. Blood dried and crusted all over me, and my wrapper in shreds. My insides, a morass. Hurtled through this forest that I saw, that first awful night, when I and my friends were snatched from the school.

The sudden pah-pah of gunshot in our dormitory and men, their faces covered, eyes glaring, saying they are the military come to protect us, as there is an insurrection in the town. We are afraid, but we believe them. Girls staggered out of bed and others came in from the veranda, where they had been sleeping because it was a warm, clammy night.

The moment we heard *Allahu Akbar, Allahu Akbar*, we knew. They had stolen our soldiers' uniforms to get past security. They pelted questions at us – *Where is the boys' school, Where is the cement kept, Where are the storage rooms.* When we told them we did not know, they went crazy. Then, some others ran in to say they could not find any spare parts or petrol in the sheds, which led to argument.

They could not go back empty-handed or their commander would be furious. Then, amid the clamour, one of them with a grin said, 'Girls will do,' and so we heard an order for more trucks to be despatched. One girl took out her cell phone to call her mother, but it was instantly snapped from her. She began to cry, others began to cry, pleading to be let home. One went on her knees saying 'Mister, Mister,' which enraged him, so that he began cursing and taunting us, calling us names, saying we were sluts, prostitutes, that we should be married and soon we would.

We were separated into batches of twenty and had to wait, jabbering and cleaving to one another until the order was given to vacate the dormitory at once and leave everything behind.

The driver of the first truck outside the school gates had a gun to his head, so that he drove zanily through the little town. There was no one about who might report on a truck passing through, at such an ungodly hour, with girls crammed into it.

Soon we were at a border village that opened into a landscape of thick jungle. The driver was told to stop and minutes after he was brought out, we heard a barrage of gunfire.

Other drivers have arrived and there is wild talk and conferring as to which girls to put in the different trucks. Terror had paralysed us. The moon that we lost for a time reappeared high up in the sky, its cold rays shining on dark trees that stretched on and on, bearing us to the pith of our destination. It is not like the moon that shone on the dormitory floor, picking up our clothes, but leaving our copybooks, our satchels and our belongings, as we were told. I hid my diary, as it was my last link with my life.

But we had not lost hope. We knew that by then the search parties would have begun, our parents, our elders, our teachers all in pursuit. Through the open sides of the truck we throw things out, in order for them to trace us – a comb, a belt, a hanky, scraps of paper with names scrawled on them – *Find us, find us.* We talk in whispers, and try to give each other courage.

We enter dense jungle, trees of all kinds, meshed together, taking us into their vile embrace. Nature had gone amok here. The terrain underneath is so rugged that even the motorcyclists, who have been riding along to stop us from escaping, keep losing their grip and are thrown onto high embankments. Rebeka says to me, 'Let's jump for it,' but I hesitate. She says, 'Better die than be in their hands.' She has been praying to God ever since we left that school and God has told her that these are bad men and that we must flee. Seconds passed and I still see it as in a mirage, that gap between two trucks, Rebeka grasping an overhanging branch, swinging from it, and then jumping. I thought, she is somewhere on that ground, dead, or maybe not dead. My nerves failed me and moreover, one of the leaders bellows, 'If any one of you jumps, you will be shot.' They must have assumed that she was dead.

The trucks lurch on and we are jolted hither and thither. Aisha, who had dozed for a moment, comes awake, shouting her mother's name. Wrenched from a dream, she starts to cry. Someone puts a hand over her mouth, otherwise we will all be beaten. We are terrified. We have nothing more to throw out. We had gone too far to be traced.

*

There is only Babby and me now. She cries from the pit of her empty belly, hoarse savage cries and I say to her, 'You have no name and no father.' I bark at her. Sometimes I want to kill her. My breasts are the size of egg cups and she is tugging at the nipples, as if she too wants to kill me. We search for a well, because the water in the ditches is brown and muddy. It tastes foul. We drink the clear water in the cavity of the big rocks. I cup my hands in it and she laps it up eagerly, swallows it, as if she might choke. Those are our moments of grace, fresh water, a little reprieve from thirst and hopelessness. I have no notion of what day it is, or what month, or what year. All I know is that the air is scudded with sand, sand blowing in from the Sahel, that scrapes our eyes and half blinds us.

Where there are no trees, the earth is an ochre yellow, scored with deep zigzag lines, quite a picture, and the young curled leaves are starting to sprout on the tips of the branches. In the night, when I lie awake, I see sky. A vast violet expanse of sky, a land of beauty that has become a place of woe. So many dead girls. The sad soughing of the trees.

I lay her down, with her head pillowed on a bit of raised turf. It is the only time she sleeps. I sleep in snatches, for fear of what might befall us. Sometimes I wake in a dream with wet eyelids, a dream of a person I must have known or even loved. But this is not the time for either memory or pathos. Occasionally I hear the barking of dogs in the distance. I have not sighted a single human being in days, and I fear that when I do, we will be dragged back for the bloodiest end.

I am unable to pray in my old tongue, as they bombarded us with their prayers, their edicts, their ideology, their hatred, their Godliness.

IT WAS A BIG, MUDDY YARD, full of clutter. Buckets, shovels, crates, wheelbarrows, paving slabs, cement and cycles. The sand is a dirt yellow from rain. There was the steady hum of generators.

Beyond the high clay ramparts, topped with loops of barbed wire, the vastness of the forest. It was dark and eerie, a multitude of trees, spawning more trees, more darkness, final banishment. The small mosque had a shiny aluminium minaret and nearby a black flag flapped from a pole. Akra, a girl from a class higher up than me, came from the dormitory where we had been held and she stood very quiet, drinking in our grim surroundings. There were only fifteen of us from our school. Others had been taken to different camps in the forest. We were flung into a dormitory of girls still asleep, and we huddled together.

A big tree dominated the centre of the compound with one stout limb forking out. It was a wet brown with a greenish tinge and I wondered if our tree at home had the same damp greenish hue. I did not know it yet but this tree was our future school house. We would stand and sit and kneel under it five times a day for prayer. We would be made to learn and memorise suras in a tongue that was alien to us and worship a God that was not ours. We would be photographed from time to time, so that the pictures would be sent back, us in our drab clothing and our numbed expressions, grouped together for distraught parents to pore over and search for their own among the many faces that now looked identical and pitiable.

From the several circular huts men appeared, hurrying to the mosque. They were dressed variously, some in jeans and T-shirts, others in baggy attire and still others with army jackets. As they ran past us, a few took us in, appraising our juiciness.

As the drone of prayer carried out to where we were, a young girl came staggering across the yard and stood before us. She shook uncontrollably. She had a thick wad of lint attached to her bottom lip that was seeping with blood. She could not speak although she strove to. She kept pointing to her mouth and finally managed to prise it open. Her tongue was gone. What crime had she committed.

While we were there, a woman in green wellingtons came towards us carrying a thorn stick. The thorns were the red of ripe berries and sharp as nails. We are ordered back to the dormitory. Thus began our initiation.

Each girl was given a uniform, identical to that which girls who had been there long before were wearing. We were told to put them on. They were a morose blue, with still darker hijabs, and though I did not see myself as there were no mirrors, I saw my friends, transformed, suddenly old, like bereaved nuns. I saw Teresa, and Fatim, and Regina, and Aida, and Kiki, all silenced, and choking back tears. We were told to gather up our old clothes, and leave nothing whatsoever behind. In the scramble, I managed to hide my little notebook. It was a teeny notebook, meant more for sums than for letters, but I squeezed words into each little square. I hoarded them. They now were my only friends. I had won the notebook, along with a scented sheet of paper, for my essay on nature. The sheet of paper had 'Woods of Windsor' written on the margins. I did not know where Windsor was.

Our clothes were piled onto a heap and no sooner had she struck the match and thrown some diesel in, than the flames shot up towards a milky dawn. Our white blouses, our uniforms and our headscarves soon dissolving into weightless flakes of grey ash that hovered for a moment, and were then borne up to find their way through the spaces, in the looped wire. I followed them in my mind, and foolishly thought that the ashen flakes would be the messengers for us. They would reach our school, where the plumes of smoke still smouldered from the fire that the militants had started just before the trucks drove away. I imagined many foolish things. I had not slept. The stench of the shoes lingered, because they took longer to burn. The smell recalled the skins of different animals in the slaughterhouses next to the markets, hung up for curing – pigs, yearlings, goats and sheep.

Then we were marched across, to sit under the big tree. Water plopped from the leaves and the ground was wet. Girls who had been there longer than us were waiting, some with their hands folded, and enraptured.

Three men get out of a cream-coloured Jeep. Two are masked and walk behind the third, who is the chief emir. He is holding a sacred text. All three are armed. As the emir comes closer to us, he stretches his hand out wide and it is as if he has snagged the entire world in his grasp.

Girls who have already seen him look up in awe and fresh wonderment. Some stretch their hands out, merely to imagine touching the cloth of his jacket. They worship him. He moves among us, recognising the new faces, his eyes so alert, as if he is seeing into our minds, into our torn hearts.

'The disease is ignorance.' He would say it three times. I did not look at him, because he was so fierce. Then he welcomed us as the emergent daughters of Allah and said that we must thank Allah for the miracle of having saved us. We may, as he said, feel estranged, but very soon the scales would fall from our eyes.

Then he lambasted those we had been taken from. Infidels. Thieves. Our president, our vice presidents, our governors, our police were all rotten. They were sultans of the banks, trawling their wealth, sitting in their big villas, on their golden thrones, watching Western movies on their big television screens. Their fat wives had accrued so much money, so much gold, so many pearls, that they had to build extra dwellings to contain this hoard. Even Muslims among these people were contaminated, drawn into that miasma of corruption. We would soon realise that the education we had received was all wrong, just as university education, which we aspired to, was all wrong. It could not be.

He asked us then to look back on the last forty-eight hours and marvel at the transformation that had been wrought. It was like he was looking into our minds and daring us to contradict him. 'When our column entered your school two nights ago, your military had pulled out because they knew we were coming. Can you trust these people? Can you trust people paid to guard you? If you are really honest your answer will be no. They could have mounted a counter-attack but they did not. They are too afraid of us. They know they will never enter Sambisa. They will never find you. They know that Allah intended for us to bring you here. As you were gathering your books and your satchels to take the transport to the school for your examination, Allah was watching, it was all predestined. Where were your pastors, where were your guardians, where were your teachers? It was ever thus. When the Prophet Muhammad was chased from Medina, his erstwhile followers looked away. Cowards. Infidels. Your parents may think they loved you and treated you kindly, but they are blind, blinded. The disease is ignorance. There is no deity except Allah. Ask forgiveness for your parents' sins and Allah will know if you are sincere in your purpose or not. Remember you have been reborn into another life. Even if you think you love your family and have made a promise in your heart, you must renounce it, you must stamp it out now. For a little while, you will shed girlish tears, but they will cease and you will be flying like birds to the fields of paradise. Angels await you, the Angel Gabriel, the Angel Azrael, the Angel Michael. Oh yes, our earthly technology and communication assisted us, but Allah informed us of everything, even the little tittle-tattle in your dormitory. I am speaking directly to each one of you. Turn to the Qur'an, turn to the Hadiths of the Prophet, anywhere you are, turn to Allah. Otherwise we will have to compel you and we will not shirk from punishments. Meanwhile, go about your daily tasks with happiness, memorise the suras, keep yourself nicely fragrant in the knowledge that you are being recruited into the vast, invincible army of Allah. You are warriors. This land that is called Nigeria must be rid of the infidels and the unbelievers. You will play your part in the fight. You will take pride in it. Even if you die on the battlefield, remember that the death of a believer is the sweetest thing. They will roll out the red carpet for you in Paradise. And now I come to the most crucial matter of all. Do not turn away. Do not be afraid. We must take the fight to the barracks of the pigs and the rats and the unbelievers that are also your own people, your own tribe, your own parents. Eat out the heart of the infidel. Eliminate them. Cut their throats. Tell them if they want you back then to bring back our dead brothers.'

Then, just before he is escorted away, he looked towards the sky, and a fleet of waiting enemies – 'Don't think you can oppose us with your jet fighters. The Allah we worship lives above your jets, poised for the instant to crush you.'

Everything in my mind went black. I had never imagined such power, such immunity. Buckets and crates rolled along that yard and the heavens parted. I saw two Gods holding staffs, or perhaps guns, outfacing one another.

The earth on which I knelt was strewn with half-eaten hearts, and there were cut throats littered everywhere, the blood gurgling away like an endless stream. I ran among the heaped remains, until I found my parents and my brother. I kissed them and they forgave me, even though they were dead. I was too sad to cry.

A few of my friends came across to ask me what was wrong. I could not answer. The small grip I had on reason was gone. We would have cut our own throats if we had knives.

'Don't worry . . . Our parents will find us,' Aisha said to me, but she had not yet been to the field of the dead.

Three girls were put to one side and stood, confused, while other women took us across the yard, towards the huts, for our next punishment.

IT WAS LIKE THE CORRALLING of cattle. We were brought out and put standing under the big tree, shivering, silent. We had been separated since we arrived. I was in a hut with a leader's wife, a shrew, who wakened me several times at night and made me repeat prayers and verses that she had taught me in the day.

When I came out and saw my friends, dazed like me, their faces distorted and pulpy from crying, I thought, I am with my friends, it won't be so bad.

Very soon men began to foregather. They were young and frisky. They wore jeans and variously coloured T-shirts. It was clear that something was about to happen, which involved us, so we clung together. Then two men wheeled on a table and set it down in the middle of the compound, while a third man put a white plastic bucket underneath it. Only seconds passed but we guessed. The first girl, Faith, was taken and as she lay down, two men parted her legs. The others were baying and cheering. As she began to scream, a hand was clamped across her mouth and the first of the youths had his turn with her. The others followed. It was the same for the second girl. I was third. As I lay on that table, I looked up and saw a few stars at great distances from one another, teetering in the heavens. It was not yet dark. It felt like being stabbed and re-stabbed and then a fierce yelling after he had broken into me. I said good-bye to my parents and everyone I knew.

I was hazy when I stood up. Clots of blood dropped into the bucket.

We were made to witness as other girls were brought on. The table squeaked as the men became even more heated and jubilant.

When it was over we staggered back, sore, baffled. We couldn't speak. We were too young to know what had happened, or what to call it. Fatim remembered that at her first school there was a doll that girls poked at and one girl took a scissors to the cloth gusset and said Dolly must have her operation. We had our operation. They had the first of us. It was dark now and stars were feasting in the heavens.

THE WOMAN LED ME ACROSS to the cookhouse. This was where I would work. It smelt of slaughter. Sides of bush meat hung from the trees outside, hosts of flies hovering and feeding on it. I had to cook for the entire unit. Commanders were to be given the largest portions, the lieutenants next and the recruits would make do with a kind of stew, small cuts of meat, with millet or sorghum added to it. When there was not enough meat I was brought strips of hide to roast. The sizzle of it, in that yard spitting out its fat and its juices made them wild with impatience. The three dogs that were locked up by day howled and hurled themselves against the galvanised door.

They had porridge in the morning, which they would eat from a trough on a big table. In the evenings, the elite would be served in their different quarters, and the lower ranks ate at that same big table. I must never serve them. Wives carry dishes from the cookhouse to the huts. If, by any chance, any one of the men should have to come into the cookhouse, I must avert my eyes.

John-John was the only boy I could meet, probably because he was so young. He was about ten or eleven. He rode a push bicycle, wore short pants and a blazer with brass buttons that were far too big for him. He rolled his sleeves up when he got down to work, and he sang. He sang with the voice of a girl. There were meats of every kind, birds and bats and lizards, the eyes of the birds staring at us, glassy, and the wild bats with their wide wings still spread out, as if even in death they remembered their night flights.

We hacked the haunches of meat and with different knives scraped the dead insects and maggots stuck to the skin. We stuffed the birds with leaves, to stifle the bad smells. He knew their names – turmeric, juniper, baobab.

I could never catch the words of John-John's song but I guessed that it is a hymn. He cycled around to the various encampments, delivering the provisions, and lived in a sort of cave with four other boys. Later, he helped me carry the big pots to the fires that we had made in the yard. They swung on chains that were attached to wooden pivots and the rotten smell of boiling meat and boiling game filled the environs of that place. It got that I had the key to the store room and unbeknownst to the wives, I could filch a few things for John-John and me to eat. He loved potato skins more than anything else, especially with roasted onions. We ate outside, where the sentries rarely patrolled, because they were afraid of rats.

Oh my God
Oh my God
Oh my God
You deserve our praise

At last, I learnt how he came to be captured:

They are coming. They are coming. They surrounded our village and we were very afraid. My sister, my mother and me. There are lots of other ladies and girls, all crying, like us, and we flee for our lives. The Jihadis surrounded our village and so we had to run. My father was not with us. He was away at the farm and we did not know if they had caught him. We ran. The other ladies who were escaping with us did not want me because I was a boy and they knew it was boys the Jihadis wanted, to turn them into soldiers. Even running we are terrified that they will chase us deep into the forest. After we have run a long time and no more breath, we fall on top of one another. Everybody is crying. My mother begs a lady to give her a dress from her bundle, so that she can make me into a girl. The lady says no. It is her best dress. Mama begged and begged and finally other women plead, say it is a matter of saving a life, a child's life. There is arguments. Then one woman pulls the dress from the bundle and she and the lady have a fight, big fight, until the dress is confiscated.

My mother takes me behind a tree, removes my short pants and then puts a blue headdress on me. They all look at me dressed as a girl and even though they are unhappy, the children can't help laughing and making fun of me. Soon it is night and we lie down wherever we can and I sleep in the blue dress. It is cold in the night. We waken very early and my sister is gone. She is nowhere. My mother goes among the groups asking for a sign of my sister and when there is none she runs around screaming and calling. But the leader of our group says it is better that we move on, because by now the militants will have learned where we are and they will be coming to kill us. All the time my mother is shouting my sister's name, 'Umi, Umi, Umi,' as if my sister will appear from nowhere. So against her will we all carry on and I can feel my mother's grief come right through me, because she has backed me. She is barely able to hold me.

We arrive at a village and there is a thatched house where everyone has huddled to escape the sun. My mother lets me down and asks another lady to mind me, because she has to find her little girl, even if it be her dead body that she finds. I see her hurry back towards the mountain. So we wait there and some people give us yam from their farm. We eat it raw. Everyone is very quiet and very afraid and no one is talking, because we do not know what next. Different rumours are whispered. After a night and another day and almost another night, my mother returns with my sister on her back and as she lets her down, my sister is saying 'Maam-ma,' because she is still afraid from the time alone on the mountain. My mother is so tired from the search and then the trudge that she falls asleep while she is still talking. 'Why did you run away?' I am cross with my sister, because she took my mother from me. She says she doesn't know why. Others were going up a hill and she followed, because she thought that we would be following behind. Then the group got scattered. Some were walking faster than others and she had to rest a little bit and then catch up with them along the mountain, so as to get across the border before day. My mother found her all alone and asleep, her clothes wet from the dew.

We stayed in the thatched house, where more lost people kept arriving. It was suffocating. Then my mother went in search of someone who had a motorbike. Before going, she undid the knot at the end of her wrapper, where she kept the little money she had saved. That money was earned from beans that we planted and sold at the market. She only took enough to pay for the motorcycle, because she knew he would want it all. She pinned the naira to the inside of my vest.

On that motor ride there were three of us, my sister, my mother and me, and we crossed underneath the mountain, where my sister nearly died. The bike was going zigzag zigzag and my sister was screaming and my mother held onto us for dear life. When we got down a slope and onto a plain, there were men loading food and water onto lorries. My mother knelt before them and pleaded for something to eat for the children. They could hear our stomachs rumbling. Her hope was to get us back to our own village, where there would be some people and maybe our father would be home by now. The men loading the lorry gave us a bottle of orange. We took turns with it. We drank very little, so as not to be greedy. The men said that the militants had moved on and so my mother decided to first go to our own farm and see if there was anything left of the harvest. Along the way, she put my sister with my grandmother, who had been hiding for weeks with cousins. The cousins did not want my sister. But hearing the sad story, her nearly dying on the mountain, they took pity and let her in. My mother and I went on to a place not far from our farm and she paid the motorcyclist and we walked up the crooked path to the top of the hill. Our crops had not been stolen, though other crops all around had been pillaged. So we picked all the beans and put them into bags that we had brought. Now we had something to sell. We headed back towards the village. A man stopped us on the path. At first we thought he was one of the Sect, but then he said a prayer that we knew, and we felt safe. He was a tall man with very keen eyes. 'Are those beans for sale?' he asked. 'Some are,' my mother replied. 'How much?' 'Five thousand naira,' my mother said and I piped up and said, 'Six thousand,' and there, on a ridge of rocky land, we bargained and bargained, so that the price shot up and in the end it had gone from five thousand to seven thousand.

Once we had rested a few days with my grandmother and the cousins and shared some of the beans, my mother decided that we must find our father. We must be a family again. With the little money, she was full of hope, believing it would enable us to start to build a house. So we took to walking, Mama backing my sister, who was clinging to her and saying 'Maama-ma' in case she was lost again. In a village we enquired of a policeman who said my father was not dead. He had heard that my father had come back to his own house and was living in one end of it that had not been completely burnt.

My father could not believe it when we walked into our half-

burnt kitchen. He was in his shirtsleeves. He holds us in a huddle, not sure if we are living or dead. He asks God if he is dreaming.

Then my mother and he sit on the floor and count all the money. They decide that in a few days, they will go back to the farm, to gather the rest of the crop. My sister was put in the church, where the pastor has taken people in, all crammed into one room and sleeping on the floor. My mother and father set out for the farm and I am alone. The idea was I would go to a neighbour in a nearby village. But I say to myself, if my parents have decided to stay all night up at the farm to guard their crops I will not go to a neighbour, I will guard our house. Then at evening time, it happens. Not on cycles. Just a boy, standing outside the window looking in at me and I knew. He had joined them. He pulled me up by the hair and out and up a bit of road where there were other boys already packed into a truck. We're riding deeper and deeper into forest, towards a mountain and one boy says to me, 'You see that mountain, it is near Pulka.'

The truck stops under trees and we are taken out and put to sleep further up. The ground is all knots. Our guards also sleep, their guns by their sides, ready. When they are well asleep and snoring we whisper:

> *Oh my God*
> *Oh my God*
> *Oh my God*
> *You deserve our praise*

One boy thinks we cannot be too far from Pulka. That is all he knows. We have overheard one of our captors on his phone saying that they are not intending to move on for four days, because of some security scare. On the third night, we will make our escape. We have to go gently. We must not run. No one must make noise. With God's grace we would make it. The boy said we would not meet a snake or a wild animal because one boy heard that the wild animals had fled the forest on account of gun battles and bombs. In the day when they make us work, gathering firewood, cleaning their cycles and their weapons, we know that they are watching us, but they do not know that in private we are praying. They give us meal in a bowl once a day. We scoop it with our hands. It is soaked in water. It is not like my mother's meal, soaked in milk. It is not enough to fill us, but we have God's grace and we are three friends together, going over the mountain to reach Pulka. We do not know anyone in Pulka, but we will ask and someone will help us. We will find our mothers and our fathers in whatever kind of makeshift home they have made. There will be a pastor in a church in Pulka and he will have contacts with many and diverse people. When they are at prayer and not paying any attention to us, we sing the song to ourselves.

> Oh my God
> Oh my God
> Oh my God
> You deserve our praise

It gives us courage. When they are sleeping, we practise crawling, and remember that we must not step over any one of them in the dark. They must not hear us running, otherwise they will go Bang Bang and we are finished. We pretend we are snakes crawling on the dirt ground. One of the boys said he ate snake, he and his family ate snake after their father cut the head from it. Their father was getting his own back on the snake world, because he had been bitten once and only that he was brought to the clinic where they had anti-venom, otherwise his father would have died. So they roasted the snake and ate it. It did not taste bad.

We had food. We hid for two days and two nights, far back from the road. We knew they would be following. On the third day, we plucked up our courage and went near the roadside, but still undercover. We were nice and clean because we had found a stream to bathe in. We drank from it. A lorry came full speed at a bend and the leader of our group bolted out, to stop it. It was carrying live chickens. There was a terrible crunch when the lorry stopped and the chickens screeched. There were two men in it. We asked them to help us. We told our story but we were not believed. They got out and told us we had to strip. They said we could be suicide bombers and no matter how we pleaded or protested our innocence, we had to do it. It was not nice, standing there naked and big men looking at us. Finally, we were told to put our clothes back on and they threw us in along with the chickens, who went fluttering and flying about.

It was a day of holy Convocation in a big church. We could hear the singing from a distance. The prophecies of the Messiah were being fulfilled. They dropped us there and people in the church allowed us in. The singing and the preaching made me cry, made me think of Sundays in church at home and my mother and all the ladies in their flowered dresses. Afterwards, we were brought to a tent and given food and Fanta. It was on account of all that praying and singing that my cousins were located, the same cousins where my grandmother had been put. They were surprised at my being brought and my grandmother wept and took me on her lap. They said I would have to sleep in the same room as her and she gave me a sign to show how unhappy she was with them.

One Sunday, they killed a chicken and ate it for their dinner. My grandmother and I got the purply bits of gizzard. We were not even invited to sit at the table with them. My granny whispered to me, 'We're not wanted here,' and that was when she hatched her plan. We would leave. We would go in the night when they were fast asleep. She had bits of furniture that she wanted to bring with her, there was a wooden calabash, spoons, a chair and a table with a lick of yellow paint. She could not be parted from them. We stole out at night and kept to the hills so as not to be seen. My granny couldn't walk very well, so I backed her. I couldn't carry the furniture and her together, so I brought her to a secluded place and told her not to move while I went back to get the things. On the way back in the dip between two *big hills, I saw the lights of the cycles bounding towards me and before I could hide from them, one was already picking me up by the hair, laughing, laughing. Then I was squeezed in between them, calling out, 'Granny . . .Granny,' and they laughed more.*

My granny died in that field and her furniture is elsewhere, rotting.

AND THE LEAVES of the trees are for the healing of nature.

My mother is crying. With joy. She is in the front row. She is wearing her best Sunday wrapper and headdress. I have been given a prize for my essay on trees. I am asked to read it aloud to the entire class and to my teachers. The prize is perfumed paper, lemony in colour, with words printed along the margins – 'Woods of Windsor'. The paper is decorated with flowers, small sprays of snowdrops in folds of green leaf. It has been rolled into a scroll, with a purple ribbon around it.

I am trying not to be nervous. I know that my friends are laughing at me and also they are jealous:

In our country we depend on trees for our lives. For shelter in rain and for shade in sun. For food of many kinds. They are our second home. Every part of a tree has its purpose. Some, such as mahogany, have oils that both cool and heal hurt skins. Many have leaves that make a savoury sauce for various dishes. Different leaves are brewed to make different flavoured teas. These induce calmness and help nerves. Then there are fruits so varied, so juicy and so succulent. In the kernel of these fruits other nourishments are hidden away, including a paste to make butter from. No one starves, because the whole year round, our trees anticipate our wants. But the most important aspect of the tree is the Tree Spirit. Ancestors who have died live there and govern lives. They ward off evil. If these sacred trees are harmed or lopped or burnt, ancestors get very angry and sometimes take revenge. Crops fail and people go hungry. 'Don't step on the spirits,' my brother Yusuf would say when we did spells in there, tiptoeing over the bony roots that wound and knitted together. It was always at evening time. Birds did not roost there, but at certain times sang some song that was both inexplicably sweet and melancholy.

My mother's tears have turned to blood. My father stands at the back, his hands folded over the crown of his head. *What are they doing to you?* he asks, his voice as deep as the morning I last heard it. His eyes are pools of an immense brown, with a well of fire in them. He is preparing to kill my captors.

I come awake on the cookhouse floor, where I must have fallen asleep out of exhaustion. I start to scrape at the clay like an animal scraping to get out. I will never get out. I am here forever. I am asking God to please give me no more dreams. Make me blank. Empty me of all that was.

I WAS CROSSING THE YARD with a girl called Hadja. She did the washing for the wives and sometimes I was told to help her. We each had either handle of the big tub, with the washing in it. She pointed to the clothesline at the far end, on a hillock, which was not far from where they buried their dead. For all their bravado, they were superstitious. They believed that their dead oversaw everything and emboldened them in battle. A girl, who had gone into trance once and predicted that a great number of their battalion would be wiped out, had her tongue removed because of her audacity. It was the little girl Aisha and I had seen that first morning.

'This is where you will be taken,' Hadja said, steering me to a cement house at the far end, a distance away from the grave-yard. It was called the Blue House, but it was almost black and the windows were gone. She said hunters lodged there in the old days, when the forest was still a game reserve. The inside walls were daubed with graffiti, tanks and guns and more tanks and more guns. The word OKAY sprawled in ignorant black lettering.

She was lame and had a speech impediment. She had been there many years and there was no telling the ordeals she had been through. Sometimes she told lies. I was not sure when she described men who came to her mistress's cave with the blood of infants in vanilla essence bottles. These were infants whose parents had sold them, knowing they were going to be smothered. The woman craved this infant blood, believing it imparted the gift of youth. She wanted to keep young for when her husband came. He was a commander renowned for his ruthlessness and had many wives and many children in different camps. The woman and the men haggled over the money.

'See there . . . see there,' Hadja said with a strange, serpentine glint in her eyes.

I saw a long corridor with cubicles leading off it and in each one an iron bed and a naked bulb dangling down. This is where girls were brought. This is where she had been brought. It was always before battle, to get them fired up, so that they set forth, sated and battle-maddened.

I told my friends this gruesome story and we waited, not knowing if they would come, but certain that they would.

Then it happened.

Guards seized us and we were marched across to the Blue House. There was blaring music and lights shone from different parts. Men were moiling around, a riffraff, in military attire, guns everywhere, knives hanging from their belts and their flies undone. As I passed along the corridor I saw that the bulbs had been lit above each bed.

Two guards undressed me, scoffing that I was to serve one of the elites. He had noticed me come in. The hairs all down my body stood up in terror and they leant in over me, to have a look, excited and skittish.

'She wants it,' one said and the other repeated it, his face so close to mine that I smelt the onions on his breath.

I vowed that I would tighten myself into a knot, a buried bulb, deep in the earth's hole and the elite man would claw and scrape like a badger, but he would not reach me. I would shut the doors of my mind. I was like some mad person shutting doors and windows, but even as I saw him come in, these doors and windows were thrown open. He was tall, bearded, with a manic look in his eyes. His aide took the gun from his outstretched arm, while a second one pulled his trousers down and folded them neatly. He did not speak. His power was in his silence and in his loathsome stare. As he lay above me, it was as if black tarp was blackly thrown over, smothering me, and shutting out all else. I knew that he would kill me if I did one wrong thing. I tried to accommodate my body to his needs, listening to him as he scraped and cursed, fuming that I am not open enough, that I am not conceding. My hands, of their own accord, go up to scratch him, to fight him and he erupts, still yoked to me, yelling at them to come. They knew what to do.

'Hold her down.'

'Subdue her.'

'Open her legs.'

He is still yelling it, even though they know exactly how his desires must be met. I both died and did not die. A butchery is being performed on me. Then I feel my nostrils being prised open and the muzzle of the gun splaying my nose. I know now that within minutes that gun will explode inside my head. *I will not wake from this, I will die with my scream unfinished.*

Even as he was pulling out of me he was shouting for a kettle of water, to wash.

Others came, singly or in pairs, guffawing, feeding and foraging and emptying themselves into me. There was an urgency. The lorries were hooting in the yard. Before long they had coalesced into one being, not like men with human traits. I went in and out of reasoning but I was not dead. They made sure of that. They slapped life back into me with savage swipes. To whet their pleasures. The same was happening to my friends in the cubicles on every side, yet no one cried out. Quiet as corpses. I watched the flies on that stinking ceiling, convening around the dead ones.

The last to come was alone, outraged at having been kept waiting, and indignant at the mess that met him. He decided that only my mouth was clean enough for his 'soldier' and he levered the muscles of my jaws with a mercilessness.

Finally they were gone. I heard lorries pass through the open gateway, amidst triumphant yodels and cheers.

I sat up and wiped my face with my wrapper. Beyond the

window the mass grave was drinking in its quota of dew and I wished that I too had died.

From the cubicles all around there is a deathly silence. My friends, like me, are sitting on their beds, waiting to see if they can stand, then face one another, and appear to be brave. There was nothing we would say, there was nothing we would ever say to one another.

Then sudden darkness as the generators are turned off and the music ceases. It is better that way. We will not have to look each other in the eye when we assemble in the corridor.

It was dark in the yard. We had banded together, but we were also alone, alone in a solitude so deep that it would never leave us. There was fog everywhere, in the sky, in the air and in our benumbed selves. Fatim teetered on her legs like a little Bambi and said that if she was going to have a baby it would be a girl, and that she would name it Jesus. Jesus would be a lady.

Those who were already asleep in the dormitory muttered their annoyance at being wakened. A few got up out of curiosity and in the fidgety gleam of one torch they saw us, our hands across our wrappers in shame, and they looked back coldly, they who had known much worse, because they had been there much longer.

When I lay face down on the mat, a girl next to me touched my hair just barely. She had nuts in her fist. She cracked them into small pieces and we ate them, almost in silence. Her name was Buki. It is how we became friends.

BUKI, SHORT FOR BUKOLA. *Bukola, a blessing from God.* They lived in a village not far from the Mandara hills. Her father had a small farm and along with farming, he went fishing every other weekend and stayed with other local fishermen in a tent. He sold some of the fish to a big hotel that had been newly built. As part payment, they were allowed to have two dinners in the hotel, where they were served yam porridge with lots of fried egg, and lemon sorbet afterwards. Her mother was not with them. Her mother had left while she was still a young child, went back to the South because it suited her better. The North, her mother said, were cattle breeders and she was used to a finer life. Her father reared her. Loved her:

One evening, just before dark, he came back from the farm to find me in a huddle with other girls from villages all about. Young men were lined up in a different group, also about to be taken. In the centre of the compound a pit had been dug and the old people, men and women, were packed in there, pleading for their lives. My father had a few naira inside his shirt, which he took out and gave to the Jihadis for my release. They took the money and then threw him into the pit with the older people, who had witnessed what he had tried to do and who despised him for it. Horses were brought on, the riders both spurring and holding them back. The horses were hesitant at first. They smelt blood. They smelt death. Their eyes were rolling, wildly. Once the pit was covered over and the horses led on top, they were made to prance. They soon got to like it, their hooves clipping off one another, and in minutes they were delirious with the exceeding joy and frenzy of their task.

My father did not get to look at me. He always said that when you are gone, it is the soul that stays behind. He said the soul weighs nothing, being of divine origin.

BARBED WIRE ABOVE US and all around us in crazy convolutions. Loops of it on the ground to trip us up. It was called the swamp. It was where we went to ease ourselves, very early in the morning, while the men were still at prayer. An abandoned putrid patch, full of flies and mosquitoes, with tall grasses and half-grown trees.

We each searched for a place to be private, for although we were sluts to them and loathsome in our own eyes, we clung to the last tatters of decency. Each girl sought a private corner and afterwards a puddle or a stream to wash in. We were each praying for our menses to come. Girls ate roots or leaves so as not to be pregnant. The crimson glitter of blood on those high blades of grass was our one deliverance. I would stare at mine and give thanks. I thought of my mother and if I were at home, how she would be fussing over me with warm water and a towel, telling me it was nature's course. I saw our kitchen, every iota, even down to the motes of dust swirling through the air and the hardened dust that had settled. I could never tell how far I was from her and from everything. The swamp was the only home we knew. It was where we tried to befriend one another.

Some of the girls from our school began to grow strange and withdrawn. The mad malaise of the compound had got into them. They were like sleepwalkers, distant, muttering and locked into themselves.

Spies skulking everywhere.

One morning a woman soldier came hurrying up the hill. Rumours had circulated that girls were plotting to escape. She had been sent to warn us. Many years before, she too had been abducted, along with four children, and a group of mothers, also with children. They had been taken from their village when the men were away. They were made to walk through dense forest, with nothing to eat except leaves and ditch water to drink. Each night, while their captors slept, they prayed and then tried to steal away, except they were soon caught. Allah had decreed their fate. They could not know at that time how enamoured they would become by their new life and how transformed by true enlightenment.

She spoke to each one of us, her eyes dancing with elation – 'If you try to escape, you will be brought back. You will be locked for three days in a detention cell. You will urinate there, you will defecate there, then, soiled and besmeared, you will be brought out for your public lashings. Next time you will not be so lucky.'

Then she was gone.

*

Down in the yard there was some cheering. The three girls who had been separated from us early on were now seated on the back of motorcycles, and dressed for travel, their hijabs folded so winsomely about their faces, like princesses. The riders were standing impatiently, as if on stirrups, raring to go.

'They're going to be sold as brides to rich men in Arabia,' Orpah whispered, and the rumour circulated. The Sect did it with the prettiest girls, to refurbish their coffers.

Orpah had been my friend from school. We made the long walk together home each evening and sometimes raided the orchards of the community centres. She had a knack of doing it, with a stick. I made a signal to her, but she ignored it. Not one of them acknowledged us. Instead, they looked away, to their new charmed lives, into an enthralled distance.

THE RAIN WAS TORRENTIAL. It was as if the sky could not disgorge itself quick enough and the ground was all squelch. Our flip-flops sank in it. It was very early. All of a sudden there was a command from a loudspeaker. We were to assemble at once beside the mosque. We thought it was an air raid and that our soldiers had come to rescue us, because although we were slaves we were also ransom money and could be bartered for big sums. They had rehearsed us in this. They had built bunkers underground and one day we were brought in small groups, put down there and buried. It was all dark and maggoty like a graveyard. We were unable to speak a word.

As we came across the yard the sight that met us was like nothing we had ever seen or imagined. A pit had been dug and earth flattened all around it. Men were gathering as for some great spectacle. Two other men, who we learned later were undertakers, stood stiffly at either side. Different workers wheeled on barrows full of stones, which were heaped and mute and malign. They were of every colour, grey, black, charcoal, with slashing edges, and had been especially picked for what was to be. There was a curious hush as before some-

- 43 -

thing ominous. The woman was led forward, and also pushed from behind as if she were a mule. She was the most beautiful woman in the whole compound. She was wife of the chief emir and word went around that she was about to be stoned for adultery.

I saw her one day in the little shop, where I had been called to unpack boxes, the booty just brought in from a village that the Sect had sacked. She was allowed first choice of the finery and trinkets and clothing. Slowly she drew on a gaud of bracelets, fiddled with them and admired them one by one. She was a haughty woman. A servant held a mirror up in order for her to admire herself. She laughed at the image of her own beauty and the status of being the chosen wife.

Then, men measured her and slid the rod down the pit, to ensure that the measurements coincided. They were very particular about it. She looked out at the miserable surroundings, the men, maybe even her husband, lesser commanders, wives, concubines and menials, almost abstractly. Then she was lowered into the pit, invisible to all except for her head and neck, which slotted perfectly above the rim.

The excitement was mounting. Men jostling and pleading to be given the honour of throwing the first stone. At the exact beat of a wooden clacker they all rushed to the heap of stones and aimed at her. The first stone struck, then bounced off the nape of her neck and she staggered within the confined place where she was held. She tried to elude the stones as they were being pelted at her from all sides, one side of her face all bloodied and then washed in the rain. She quailed helplessly. The stones were coming pell-mell, falling monstrously on what was once the most legendary face in the enclave. Strips of the other side of her jaw came hanging off and when she screamed, those screams transformed in the victorious yells of her executioners.

I wanted her to die, instantly, to be dead before they could deface any more of what had been, but broken as she was, she did not die yet, and her eyes flinched violently. She tried to move her head again and again, to escape her fate, and struggled to get her hands out in a last futile gesture of despair. But the slaughter was relentless. The blood was pumping heartily out of her veins. The stones themselves were smeared as they fell, but presently were picked up, to continue the onslaught.

She was like some ghoul now, a mimicry of who she once had been, bleeding on one side and shredded on the other. The men roared in triumph. It was evident that she was almost gone and her eyes, which she had shut tight in a clench, opened to a knowing, aghast goggle, before the neck hung off, heavy and harmless. The stones themselves, the accomplices of the act, were thrown onto the wheelbarrows, to be kept in readiness. The strangest thing of all was her hair, so long and luxurious, it seemed to bristle with life.

THE CAMP WAS ALMOST DESERTED. They'd gone in trucks earlier, bringing most of the girls to help with building makeshift huts in the forest, for newcomers that had arrived. I sit under the big tree to stretch my bones. I had done the preparation for the dinners. It was beef, roasting on the big fire and spitting its juices. An emir's wife had brought me a set of new knives. They were in a cutlery case, with cavities for each knife.

Then I saw four men cross the yard. He was the most noticeable, eel-thin and cocky and wore a jazzy shirt. The music from their phones is belting.

All of a sudden he is running ahead and I am pulled out onto the open ground. He removed my wrapper, gesturing them to take pictures on their phones and then it happens. The slash of his zipper, the blast of his breath as he moves into me to the rhythm of music. They move too and take picture after picture on their phones – my head that he is holding down with his grimed hands, my face, my clenched teeth and his dancing, arching silhouette.

There is a black void within me, but not void enough to blank everything out. I take one of the knives and rip it down the length of his body, so that he is sliced in half. But he is not dead. Their bragging, the competing gliding of their cameras have emboldened him. At moments he slides out for the camera to peer in. They feed on his prowess, his hot desire and his detestation of me. They laugh at my screams as he judders my entire body on that sad earth.

Only when the last sound has died in his throat does he take his leave of me. But it is not over. They want pictures of my face, my face on that ground, blank, aghast, emptied of life. There is an extinction of all things then, except for the shifting black blobs that swam behind my eyes.

They have hurried away and the music blares in the distance.

A girl I barely know comes and stands above me. She puts my wrapper over me to cover the shame. The top of the big tree stands patient against the sky and the leaves murmur as before rain. Then a breeze from the forest, a cool breeze that heralds rain is blowing all over my body and down along my legs like silk. The rain came in great noisy squalls, sheets of it coming down to wash everything clean. Rain is fierce and sudden and merciful. Did God send the rain or did the Rainmaker. Did God witness what happened and did he write it into his big ledger for the Day of Judgement. Oh God, empty me of him. Is that too much to ask.

Will I ever know the language of love. Will I ever know home again.

A WIFE OF THE EMIR came to the dormitory as we were undressing and said to put hands up, who had their menses. I put my hand up, as did four others, but it was obvious, as the blood ran down our legs in rivulets. The rags we used were not absorbent and we had no safety pins to secure them with.

We stood, a little embarrassed as she looked and noted our names and the mat we slept on. The next evening more hands went up and by the following day we were nine in all. We guessed what it was for. A husband-to-be had excelled himself in battle and the reward for that was marriage to a girl who was not with child.

In the morning we were brought for viewing. We stood in a huddle and then she told us to spread out and the young man walked among us, appraising us as if we were cattle. He was shortish, his face partly uncovered and one of his eyelids drooped. He did not look directly at anyone. Then on the third circuit, he lingered where I stood and I knew that he expected me to smile, except that I didn't. Afterwards he and the emir's wife went to another room, while we waited, unsure, because who could say which was worse, meeting the requirements of one man, or the six or seven who plundered us nightly. Then she beckoned me into another room and on the way congratulated me at how lucky I was.

She sat me down but he and I did not exchange a word. Nevertheless, we were to be married.

Afterwards, she gave me my bride money and told me to go to the store and buy things. I bought a clean cotton wrap, sanitary towels, and a packet of biscuits to share with my friends.

When I crossed to our dormitory, my friends were cold with me. Why me and not them? Buki was close to tears.

'I'll come and find you in the garden,' I whispered, but she did not answer.

The ceremony was very brief and very simple. I was put standing next to the mosque as the emir recited prayers and read verses from the Qur'an, which I repeated after him. My husband was not present.

It was dark in our hut when I met him. The bed we sat on was low and he took my hands and he put them between the palms of both his hands in gratitude. Then he told me his name, which I repeated and I told him mine. Mahmoud. Maryam. I knew that I did not love him.

He gave me a gift of a veil, which they must have looted from one of the shops in a town before torching it. It did not smell of burning. How many girls had looked at it in a shop window and dreamed of owning it and where were those dreams now. Lost in an infinite nowhere. And where were those who had dreamed them.

He was hesitant, not like the brutes, and I knew that I would have to encourage him. He removed my clothes and then his own, placing his hands all over my body, as a blind person might and that was his way of claiming me as wife. Maryam. Mahmoud.

It was lashing outside and we could hear the rain dripping off the grass fringing of the roof as we sat postponing the next minute and the next. Then just before getting into the cot bed he dragged something from under it. I thought it was a gun, as many of the others kept their guns as a boast, while they jovially raped us. Instead it was a long wired cord with metal snouts that all of a sudden pulsed into light. Lights came willy-nilly, purple and blue and magenta, all along the floor, on his hooded eyelid and on my hand that searched for his.

In the morning he touched my lips, delicately with his fore-finger and he told me his mother's name. Onome. She was the person he loved most. He had enlisted to save her from starvation. The Sect were always scouring villages to recruit young men of a fighting age, promising them big sums of money. One night, they came to his village and he was soon persuaded. He hid the money in the granary, where he knew his mother would find it, but he did not say goodbye.

'And you left her?'

'I belong here now,' he said, as if he were talking to one of his commanders.

'What happened to your eye?' I asked. And he thought for a moment before answering. As a young boy in his village, he had been caught in a skirmish between Muslims and Christians and accidentally a stone that was intended for someone else caught his eyelid and tore it.

'Can you see?' I asked.

'I can see you,' he said.

We went about our various duties and never met until evening, when I served his supper and watched, sitting a little apart, while he ate. Then I ate. Then he prayed.

'But you have not converted,' he said.

'No, I have not converted,' I replied, but I was not as afraid of him as I had been of the others.

Sometimes he was gone on raids for days, weeks, never saying where he had been or how bad the fighting was. He would return hungry for food, for comfort, for rest. In those times, back from battle and readying for the next one, he was like a dreamer, saying little, as if he wanted to separate the two worlds, the two hims. He worked over in the carpentry shed and made a shelf for above our bed, where we put the torch, my broken comb and the razor with which he trimmed his beard. He loved his beard and talked to it.

It was mayhem in the camp. A truck was driven in and the dead bodies laid out in a line, next to the mosque. Wives were allowed to search for their husbands, but there was to be no crying. Some men had their faces blown off, so that the women had to identify them by a boot or some scrap of clothing.

Mahmoud was not among the fallen. I did not love him, but I did not wish him dead.

He was brought back a few evenings later, carried into the hut and laid down. A soldier held a lantern above him and in the swaying light I saw his right leg, broken and skinless, with matter oozing from it. The male nurse who had brought him also had some ointments and bandaging, but said it would be better to leave the wound open to the air and to discourage him from itching it.

'What if his leg has to come off?' I asked.

'Then he is no longer any use for combat,' was the reply.

He lay there in a gloom, beyond reach. Sometimes he talked to himself, but he did not talk to me. The wife of one of the elders would come to dress him and I was sent out. I watched through the window hole. I watched her pour water from a plastic bowl, all over him several times, then she dried him, dried his hair and his beard, the beard that he now tugged at in the night. She brought him a soup made from scraps of meat and bone. He was so feeble he slurped it. He drank tea brewed from flowers, which she brought back from the village. Older wives, such as her, were allowed out, beyond the frontier, but I never yearned to go, because I knew that a glimpse of the outside world would break my heart.

Feeling lonely and unwanted, I used to walk around and

hope I might meet one of my old friends. One day I saw Buki in the gardens, in her khaki smock, her face scrunched, her whole being intent on pulling up tangled roots of trees, to make a new patch of garden. Twice she straightened up and lifted her face, but she did not acknowledge me. I wanted to tell her I was having a child, but that was not possible. I had told no one.

It was weeks later and still he had not recovered. His mind wandered. I could hear him talking to himself, or to this creature on his lap that he cradled, as though it were a child. I had no idea what it might be. I longed to take out the string of fairy lights that had marked our wedding night and one evening, to my surprise, he told me to get them. His leg was stretched out on a stool, but I could see that it was suppurating.

'I'm an animal . . . I am an animal,' he said, fiercely. He could not contain it any longer. His unit had raided the village he was taken from. He and three others were sent on ahead, across the sacred grove. The weathered mud huts were quiet in sleep, his mother in one of them. Within minutes, the entire settlement was crumbling. His first cousin tried to escape and when the commander saw him skulking away, he was apprehended. Mahmoud was then ordered to kill that cousin with a knife. 'Turn the knife three times,' the commander said and so he turned the knife three times, as if chopping timber.

Then his mind cracked and he began to speak senselessly, the nine daughters of some god and the image of a beheaded head. 'A beheaded head is a wild and dripping thing.' It was what he held, it was the creature that he had been conversing with all those weeks and that he cradled in his arms.

'Shut up, Mahmoud, or they will shoot you.' I knew that if they heard him he would be brought out for a beating, or worse. I kept trying to hush him. *A beheaded head is a wild and dripping thing.* He would never come back from this delirium.

'I am having a child and they will shoot us both,' I said. That shook him. He stopped his raving and told me to fetch a plastic bag from under the bed. There were folded newspapers inside it, each one containing an envelope filled with money. It was the money they had been given after successful raids, to instil in them the notion that they were free, which they were not. The notes were dirty and frayed. They smelt of flesh. I did not count them.

'But this is freedom money,' I said holding up one wad.

'Hide it . . . tell no one,' he said and he stroked my cheek in a wan memory of how we had once been.

Then he began to laugh, wild, unruly laughter. He remembered a joke. As a reward for his bravery, he was invited to sit at the front of the truck next to the driver and that way when they returned to base, he was welcomed by his comrades as a hero.

It was the last time we were together as man and wife.

THE PAINS STARTED IN the early morning. Mahmoud was not there. He lived away from me ever since the night he confided his perfidy. He slept in a hut near the rampart, along with other watchmen who were no longer any use for combat.

Once I went into labour, women were sent for. They were from villages that the Sect had taken, but they were unharmed, because of their skill at delivering babies.

There were about nine women in the group, all with guns, which they put down.

It was in an open space with a straw roof, empty rice bags on the floor to serve as cloths and full bags of cement in one corner. They brought various things – rags, pails of water, small sticks finely shaven and bundles of leaves. I learned later that the leaves were both a poultice for my forehead and also for brewing, to make a drink when the pain was extreme.

They were talking and cackling and fussing about, already arguing among themselves as to what was best to do. One woman, whose name was Rashidah, dampened my lips and told me to be brave.

The fighters were already out in the yard, shooting their

guns in the air in expectation. She told me that the real jubilation came with the birth, that is, if it was a boy. A future
fighter. If it was a girl, there was less gunfire and no jubilation.

The pain began to get worse and to ease it Rashidah dipped
the shaven sticks in a pan of water and sprinkled me with it.
Some of the others were half crazed, shouting prayers and
incantations. Every time I let out a roar, the vexed woman
gripped my hair and said it was a mother's lot. They were
running around, disputing with each other and then one put
stones on my chest, to hurry up the labour. Pepper was heated
on the fire they had made outside and then a warm paste of it
was spread over my face. I was suffocating. I began sneezing
and begged to be brought outside.

When the wall of water burst from inside me, I thought
everything would be easier and Babby would uncoil and swim
out of me like a fish and then flounder along the floor.

I am moved over and positioned on the bags of cement,
so that my buttocks are raised. It was like I was being sawn
in two. I could feel the ball of its head, like a metal hoop,
making up its mind to come out, but then retreating. This
happened many times. They said I would have to count the
time between the contractions and hold my finger up. They
counted by stamping their feet. The brew I had drunk had
made me woozy. They were shouting at me to push and then
two of the women slid their hands inside, to haul the head
out. I felt the shoulders, first one, then the other, cleaving

their way, and then I heard it bawl and vent its rage on the abhorrent place she was born into.

It came out in a wet whoosh and once the cord was severed and knotted, it was held up for me to see. It was a girl. There were hollers of dismay – 'It is not a male child.' Two women, whose job it was to announce the birth, went to the door, each holding up a black rag and the fury was instantaneous. There was no cheering, only sporadic gunshots, and men dispersing. I did not know where Mahmoud was, but wherever he was, the honour he had hoped for was not to be. Blood was oozing from me, followed by small clots that eked out in silent surges. I am moved back onto the floor, so that the cement bags would not be harmed. Then, Rashidah put a fingerful of corn into my mouth and told me to chew it and swallow it, because that child would be needing milk.

Some were complaining because the placenta had stuck. They were starving. I saw them tear it out in pieces and then sit on the floor and eat it. Others were picking up their guns and getting ready to go. Their work was done.

The shrew who had been in charge of the pepper poultice told me to clean up all that blood before I left. Rashidah stayed behind for a moment, took a syrup jar out of a bag, which had a small consignment of oil in it. She also had a taper, which she dipped into it and lit it.

I was alone with my child for the first time. Her cries spoke of some hunger and something more. She pounded on my chest. I believed she would have drunk my blood in lieu of milk, if she could get to it. I wetted her lips with water that had been left in a bowl. She spat it out. I tried holding her, but she slithered out of my grasp.

I prayed that someone would come, but no one did, not even Mahmoud. Perhaps he had been forbidden to. I am even afraid to hold her. I run to the far corners calling to anyone who might be passing outside.

Later on, I do not know when, I crawl to where she is. She looks at me, looks through me, with a vacancy.

A WHINE, A WHISTLE, then rumbling as if the earth were turning itself inside out. Our army had come to rescue us.

I could not see the plane as it was too high up, but out of the vapourish darkness, sheets of lightning were streaming down and the whole yard is a blaze of colour. It was not yet dawn.

It was as if I had already rehearsed it. I knew what to do. I picked up my child, backed her and took the wrapper with the escape money in it. 'Run. Run.'

Balls of fire swirl through the air in the yard and the militants from their trenches are shooting up, unable to deter the next bombardment. Orders are being yelled for us to go to the bunkers to which we had been assigned, but these commands are ignored. I was running through smoke and carnage, running in the direction of the fire and yet weirdly unharmed by it.

I met Buki halfway and she grabbed my arm as we ran together. We had not spoken since my marriage but that did not matter now. We had to step over the dead and the dying. Girls lying there, their cries, their cries. Cycles, laptops, fridges, umbrellas, bed springs, all flying up and then tangling in grotesque heaps onto the dead. My last sight of that blazing and hated inferno was of their black flag, with its white insignia of swords, in tatters everywhere.

Mahmoud was on sentry duty. It was the task he had been given after his leg was amputated, since he was no longer a fighter. He had not spoken to me since the night he confessed his disloyalty. He slept in a hut next to the sentry box and he and Musa, the mechanic, alternated shifts. He had never seen the child. It was I who named her. Babby.

'Go, go,' he was saying, as Musa tried to block us, but Mahmoud struck him such a hard blow that he staggered.

We were out.

Over a trench and into the first frontier of the forest. It was dark, darker still where the trees meshed overhead. Paths and slopes were wayward, but we ran with a speed we did not know we had. Our legs vaulted us.

We had run a great distance before we flopped down under a cover of trees. Old mulchy leaves beneath us, green leaves above us and our hearts hammering. Babby was asleep, as if she had died. We were unable to speak. A bird with a chestnut belly chirped ceaselessly as it stood on the ground looking at us. Fat tears fell from our eyes. Finally Buki whispered, 'We are free . . . we are free.' Not since the three girls had been taken that morning, long ago, to be sold as brides, had the word *free* escaped our lips. The leaves were still shedding water, and we raised our faces to them, to be baptised anew, to be washed clean. The shelter that flowed from those trees, so benign, so different from the tamarind tree we sat under.

We were a little hysterical. We kissed the moist mossy barks and pressed our foreheads to them in gratitude.

From the shoulder bag that she kept in the garden, Buki took things out. She was smiling at her own enterprise. She had always believed that our army would come and that she would escape. Each night she stored whatever she could steal and always filled a water bottle from the emir's cistern in his private garden.

She had nuts, a fistful of seeds and a piece of bread, which she broke in three. To anyone observing us from above we would have seemed lost and insignificant, but to ourselves we were champions. Babby held her piece of bread in her mouth and sucked on it, her sole sustenance. We pulled up tufts of grass and moss to make pillows, because the roots of those trees had spawned and were hard and sinewy. Buki and Babby fell fast asleep, but I was unable to. I was listening for the sound of the trucks coming through the forest to recapture us. Then, in half sleep, I pass through that bombed-out yard and see them pull up their own dead for burial. I see my friends dazed and distracted, walking around, searching, not knowing who or what they were searching for, but knowing in their hearts that with their bodies they would pay dearly for this bombardment. Fast asleep, I dreamt of Mahmoud, his mangled corpse, free of all obligation, reunited with his mother and his beheaded cousin.

＊

Night came suddenly, the shadows flitting at first but then thicker, sturdier. The air was full of rustles, scrapings, squealings and the terrors born of night. Buki had gone in search of food. She had been gone a long time. My thoughts were dark also. I was alone. I thought what if she did not come back. What if she went astray on one of those paths that meandered towards everywhere and nowhere. What if we never made it to the tarred road. I held Babby. It was hard to know who was mother and who was child.

'Come chop,' Buki said merrily as she came back with bunches of dates that hung from their slender branches. We ate standing up. '*Dabino. Dabino.*' We gorged. I fed Babby mouth to mouth. It was the first sweet thing she had ever tasted. She drooled for more. More. I did not love her enough. How grim her life had been from the moment she was delivered by these heartless midwives.

The plan was that we would walk at night and count to a thousand steps at a time. She had been told it by a gardener who sometimes came up from the village. However, she said that instead of counting we would sing. The words came back to her easily and jauntily.

> Mary come to house oo
> Mamma say 'Na wetin?'

Mary say 'Na fever.'

Mama call the doctor,

Doctor say 'Na fever!!!'

Mama boil some water oo

Mary go to bath oo

Hot water, hot water,

Make Mary die!!!

Hot water, hot water,

Make Mary die!

We followed what we thought was the straightest path but how could we tell. We could not even see our own hands. Big trees massed together accruing more darkness, fallen boughs, overhanging branches and posses of thorn bushes that tore at our feet.

Suddenly something furry shot across my instep. I felt its paws, its long nails and the lash of its tail as it shrieked. I also shrieked. Then came the roar of an animal, an avenging roar that was a warning to the other animals all about. They signalled back to it. Obviously, it had been caught in some trap and other animals were answering to it. Birds flew out of the trees in alarm, some with their young in their mouths, and a biggish animal passed me by, dragging a heavy trap with his hind legs. Buki was not with me. She had gone on ahead. As I tightened Babby to my back, I fell face down, clutching at earth that was only slurp. Leaves were still shaking but otherwise the place was silent as though suddenly sacked. I was crying help-lessly. Buki came after what seemed a long time. She too was grimed.

'I'm sorry,' I said, since it was my scream that had set off the furore.

'We won't walk again at night . . . We'll be babes in the wood,' she said, and hauled us up. We stood cleaved together, in the splotchy light of a hazed moon and took our first steps, puddling in slime, until we came to a path that ran between big boulders. They opened onto a wide plateau of rock that sprawled for a great distance. Grass grew on it and there were also deep hollows to shelter in. It was where we would spend the remainder of the night.

*

I fell into a heavy sleep and yet I was thinking, *We are resting now, we are gathering our courage to go on.*

In a dream I saw the roof of our house where it adjoined the granary, the cut corn spread out to dry. Would I be home in time to help with pounding it? In the very next dream my mother is sitting on a chair in the middle of a busy market, with a plate of food on her lap. She is ashamed. She is wearing a shabby, sleeveless brown dress. *But you never liked brown,* I say. She tells me that the dress has been donated. So we are poorer than when I left. She's being asked by a policeman to verify my first name, our family name and my exact age. As she begins to answer, she gets flustered and the plate falls from her lap. I waken with a jolt. Something is beating on my chest. It is Babby, her fists on my breastbone, trying to tap it open. She seems to be pleading with me, saying, *I know there is not much milk, I know there is none, but I am asking to be held.* I hold her tight, tighter. It was her sighing that moved me the most, so plaintive, so sad, like a very old, sad person. I traced my finger over her face, the skin silken and now moist, a night flower that hides by day. Then I put two fingers inside her mouth and all along her gums, feeling for where her milk teeth would sprout.

'Things will get better,' I said. I believed that she knew. In her child's way she seemed to grasp what was happening.

*

A morning mist hovered above the ground. We marched through it. We stamped on it. Our sleep had made us purposeful. We passed a clearing where black sluggish water crept out of a soggy hole and was undrinkable. Buki said that in the valley down below we would be certain to find a water hole and rivers. She had dreamt of her school days and the nice teacher who read them a fable every Friday. In her sleep the words of the fable returned to her exactly as she had heard it.

Uban da dansa. Fathers and sons:

Once upon a time there was a farmer whose newly planted farm was being destroyed by some animals. One evening the farmer set a net trap for the marauding animals, in the hope that they would bring food. When he went back the next morning he found six goats and a dog under the net. 'Release me, I beg you,' cried the dog to the farmer, 'for I have eaten none of your crops, nor have I done you any harm. I am a poor innocent dog, as you may see – a most dutiful father—' but the farmer cut him short. 'All this may be true enough, I dare say, but I have caught you with those destroying my crops, and you must suffer with the company in which you are found.'

We came on something very strange. It was by a creek, with only a little water, and the reeds soaking up what was left of it. There were stones in the middle, black and white stones crammed together. A man, spider-thin, was sitting on a fallen log. He was wrapped in a dirty sheet, like an old dressing gown and he had a plastic bag on his head to keep off the sun. He held an empty bottle in his hand, clutched it with the need of a child. At first he had seemed to us to be dead but then he took us in, his eyes staring out of his shaven skull. We knelt to show our respect, but he did not want that, so we got up.

'Is there a village near here, Uncle?' Buki asked. She had to say it three times. He gave her a cold, slighting look.

'We are just trying to get home, Uncle,' she said pleading.

'Yonder,' he said and with his bony wrist waved us away.

Nearby was a tree, struck by lightning. Not a single bud

- 68 -

or leaf clung to it. Its boughs were bleached and underneath there was the frame of a carcass of an animal. It had no smell.

As we went on down, Buki saw what looked like a grove and she ran to explore. Someone, or maybe nature herself, had tried to cultivate an orchard there. The bunches of mango were small, cheek to cheek, along the thin drooping branches. They did not have the red blush and golden skins of mangoes in the markets at home, but we ate them anyhow. They tasted sour, like pickles.

Then she took Babby in her arms and went in search of better fare.

From one enormous tree, three lesser trees had sprung, leaving a big hole in the bark that gaped like an open mouth.

'Don't,' I said but her hand was already inside it, rummaging and tossing things out – twigs, dead leaves and a brown beak, which was all that was left of some hibernating bird. Lastly she pulled out hunks of a jellied substance that she held aloft. In the light, it seemed like ropes of yellow-hued necklace. She tasted it. I did the same. It tasted medicinal. Babby spat hers out. Buki took her in her arms and said they would go on a hunt. She was more playful than I was and I secretly resented that Babby loved her more. Deep within the crusted bark of a certain tree she found amber capsules that contained drops of juice with a delicious tart flavour.

*

It was an army camp fairly recently abandoned. There were old clothes, socks and cartridge shells thrown about. There was also a water hole with a metal dipper, but no water flowed. She turned the wheel and we waited and heard a trickle and then a gush of water, deep from the earth's bounty. We drank mug after mug of it.

Behind were the remains of a building, probably where animals were once housed, and a lean-to that led to an open porch. The porch is full of boxes, metal boxes with letters in bright silver engraved on them: MRE. *Meals ready to eat.* MEALS: READY TO EAT.

We go through box after box, only to find that they are empty. But something tells her not to give up and she comes back waving a polythene pouch with a bag inside it, also with silver lettering, that tells us it contains 'Beans and sausages'. There is a cartoon with instructions on how to use it. It involves pulling a string that dangles to one side and we learn that if it is correctly applied the outside bag will open and the temperature inside will go from freezing to the desired heat. We are to allow twenty minutes' cooking time. But we dare not risk it. Anything could go wrong. Better to eat the stuff cold. She tears a folded flap along the top, but this bag is too tightly sealed. We try with our teeth, gnawing and biting, until finally she gets a stone and punches holes in it. As she does, small slivers of ice fall out. Beans are coated in a tomato sauce and the sausages, which are thick, are cut up into small chunks. We stuff ourselves. We found goggles, donned them and swanned around having imaginary talks with officers. Seeing that we were skittish, Babby also wanted to play. She was in no mood for sleep. She kept prattling and taking each of our hands to be hoisted in the air. She was so wide awake we had to take turns with her.

Buki picked up a stone and put it in one or other hand that I had to choose from. It was my turn to have the first hour of sleep. I found an old army coat with a big collar and wrapped myself in it.

*

We went on next morning, buoyant and full of purpose, until we hit a storm and were tossed about in all directions. A desert wind keened and the whirling sand swirled in a mad rage. We were shouting to one another but unable to hear. Babby was slipping off my back, like loose luggage. I dimly remembered Buki calling to me but it was too late. I am sliding down into a chamber of darkness. She too slipped as she tried to save me and fell into that crumbling pit. Our cries to one another are swallowed in swills of sand. She groped so as to test the walls to see if she could scale them, but small tussocks with wisps of grass came off in her hand.

She finds one wall where sand and mud have combined to give a slightly stronger footing. She makes grooves in it, not deep enough to settle in, just small foot holes to enable her to scale it. She makes four in all. She will go first and then I will throw Babby up and lastly I will follow.

'We have to.' That is all she says.

I watch her toe settle into the first groove and I see the frightened wobble of her heel. She reaches for a second footing, makes it and after four steps she pauses. She is trying to be jovial as she stands like someone in a circus, on a tightrope entertaining an audience. She begins to claw and make careful thrusts, until she reaches the edge, then hoists herself over and shouts down. Babby is next. I take off my wrapper and fold her tight in it. I stretch on tiptoe, higher, higher as Buki strains and reaches to catch her. At the moment she is handed over I hear her cry, a cry of astonishment.

Now it is my turn. I am ashamed of my terror. I take the first, then the second groove and feel for the tiny cavity of the third and the fourth. I am perched there, when something on the other side of fear emboldens me and drives me on. All I want is for the tip of Buki's fingers to touch mine so that I know I am safe. I do something unwise. My mind had no part in it, it was all impulse. I slid back down.

I can hear Buki gasping as she pulled and pulled to get me halfway up. The wall of sand, which I am clawing, is flaking. I cling to nothing. It is now only a matter of minutes before these walls collapse. She is no longer shouting, she has no breath left, just tugging and tugging until finally my brow is over the edge and I bite the earth. The wind has died down. Buki is standing above me, limp with exhaustion.

'I am sorry,' I finally manage to say.

'You're here,' she says, smiling.

It was the best of all knowing and feeling and forgiving.

*

We have to find water to wash as we are caked in sand. We walk a long distance and finally we come on a water hole with a gourd hanging on a piece of wire. First we drink. It tastes of clay and matter. Our thirst is so great that we drink it anyhow, we slurp it. Babby also slurps hers. Then we wash her and take turns at ladling water over our bodies. We wash our wrappers and hang them on a tree to dry.

We have been sitting for some time when suddenly we hear something in the sky. The sound is faint, like the distant buzzing of bees. We are naked, like the first man and woman in the Bible. The machine that we occasionally glimpse moves with stealth, like a glider. It is veering in our direction. We know it is not the militants as they did not have planes, so we are jumping up and down, reckless with happiness. We pull the wrappers from the trees and wave them, frantic and giddy. It dips silently over a belt of trees and towards a clearing that is almost directly above us. We are hoarse from shouting. Then just as we are expecting it to land, with men rushing out, bearing sheets or blankets, our hopes are vanquished. It dips sideways under an awning of cloud, then under massed cloud, vanishing into the distance from where it had first appeared. It had not come for us. Buki remembered that it was a drone. Countries from all over the world sent them into other countries in order to spy. They were just machines, gathering information that would be sent back, by satellite, to some alien territory.

'There was no one in it,' she said.

'So why did it come?'

'They comb the skies now . . . they're a new tactic of war.'

'But it saw us?'

'But we were nothing to them.'

We stood, our hands across our timid bodies, ashamed of ourselves.

*

We rounded a bend and saw something we had hoped never to see again. The old man was gone, the creek almost dried up, stones rasping in the heat. The reeds now yellowed with thirst. She was furious. She blamed herself. How could we have gone so astray.

'We mustn't quarrel,' I said.

'We are not quarrelling,' she said. Then she went to the tree that had been struck by lightning, determined to break off the last remaining branch. It did not want to come away. She pulled and strove. She persevered with it until her fingers bled. What came off was a stick, the flesh at its ends white and splintered. She swung it in all directions and railed at the heavens.

'Let's think,' I said.

'Of what?' she said sharply and went off.

The worst thing was the sameness, the same big trees, the same treetops, patchy light filtering through, same thorn bushes, same baked earth with no shade, and us literally dying of thirst. Never since we escaped did this forest, those trees, this vaulting sky seem so alien, so malignant, so pitiless and so indifferent to us. We were at the rim of existence and we knew it.

When Buki returned I could see she had cried her eyes out. She was staring down at the ground and scoring it with the end of her stick.

'What do you want to do?' she asked.

'I want to go on,' I said.

As we walked, in silence, I remembered a shrine we had crept into late one evening. It was hidden away in a grove, a little structure, with its door unlocked. We went in on tiptoe. Everything was topsy-turvy. There was an after-smell of burning and clay pots were broken and scattered about. We saw the charred feet of chicken legs and discoloured cockscombs. Images had been defaced. Buki said it had been vandalised. She recognised that it was where the tree worshippers came for their secret rituals in the dead of night. She said they were not evil, they were good people and yet someone wanted to harm them. They worshipped a different God from ours, but they did not kill.

Outside birds were hidden in the trees, hermit birds singing their little hearts out.

'Maybe they will come back,' I said, meaning the tree worshippers.

'They won't,' she said, with a terrible finality.

AFTER THE TRUDGE, the thorns, the hunger and our short tempers, we are reconciled. We glimpse happiness. There it was waiting for us, a little ruin smothered in wild grasses, blackish thatch sprouting from the roof. A broken chair had been left outside, as if someone had just vacated it. The door had fallen off its hinges.

Buki found it, as I had stopped to feed Babby and suddenly, through a barricade of trees, I hear her calling and I am surprised at her eagerness, since she had been so surly.

We stood on the threshold, unsure at first, and then went in. The roof leaked and the drip-drip of water onto the clay floor was a lingering entreaty. Mildew over everything, a grey fuzzy coating along the clay walls, utensils and plates overturned and a saddish orange cover across the narrow bed. She found a rush basket full of things, a scissors, a torn sheet of a magazine with pictures of paint tins and a sign that read 'Home decorating'. There was also a blanket laden with dust. She found a man's squashed straw hat and plonked it on Babby. There was a watch, which she shook and put to her ear and then put to my ear and for an instant it ticked. Then it stopped. We found a cigarette lighter in a bright red case, the wick torn and sooted. She flipped the catch again and again, begging it for just one little spark. There was a green candle in a tall bottle, with blobs of green wax crusted on the nozzle. We had no matches.

Outside, two water barrels overflowed and a stream ran down from the hills. In a shed we found a shovel, a hoe, a yard brush and grass seeds that had been packed in a jute bag.

The garden, light and sunny, was a riot of weeds and on the ground, the rotting apple butts were infested with worms. Bits of coloured wool, cloth flowers and the silver wrapping of a chocolate bar were tied on the posts, to discourage predators. In a neatly dredged patch, the purple flower of the potato blossomed here and there. She knelt and pulled a few stalks up. Some had small knots of potatoes covered in clay, which she shook off. She counted them. On black posts, some of which had fallen down, there were affectionate reminders of the previous owner. He had tried to grow a flowering shrub but all that remained were black leaves and the frayed yellowish pollen of dog roses.

We set about cleaning the kitchen. We washed the floor, the trestle table, the broken chair and the various utensils. We ran the broom up and down the walls until they were their dun colour again, the fungus gone. We took turns beating the blanket. We beat it with a fury, as if we were beating our captors and the more they cried for mercy, the harder we struck with the handle of that broom or that shovel. We washed Babby in an old tub and then washed ourselves, half gleeful, half shivering and lastly, we washed our hair and let it dry in the sun.

To make fire she needed to practise alone. When she was young, boys and girls went into the bush on Saturdays on adventures. Boys hunted hares and rabbits, while the girls searched for snails. Then they made fire by rubbing stones together and the one boy who excelled at it thought himself to be Mr Superman. The snails, as she recalled, tasted delicious, tastier than when they were cooked at home in a pan.

I sat outside on the broken chair with Babby on my lap. I had not looked at sunsets in a long time, but this sunset was a ball of copper and the sky with skeins of crimson running out of it in all directions. I felt it was specially for us.

'Look,' I said. She pointed her finger and looked but was indifferent to it.

Just before dark, Buki came, a supply of stones in her wrapper. We watched as she struck the edge of one particular stone along the side of another as nonchalantly as if she were striking a match. She had obviously practised. One little spark appeared, too wan and wobbly to survive, yet more lay in waiting. Pinpricks of gold that as she breathed on them, whooshed into life, and were then carried across in her cupped hands to the fire that she had already laid. Ribbons of flame shot up, orange and blue and violet flames feeding off one another and spluttering.

Show me the diamonds
Show me the gold
Call me the answer

Oh yeah
Call me anywhere
I don't have a care
This is my world

Buki is irrepressible, her face glowing with the light from the fire, her eyes big and black with a melting blackness. She is dancing a slow lazy dance, as Babby totters behind. Sparks fly about and the old blighted trees, with their straggling white beards, creak into life, from the blazing fire.

'*Oh pretty baby, oh pretty baby, oh pretty baby, yeah.*' The words come back to her, along with the excitement of those mischievous evenings. Once every six weeks or so, when her father and neighbours went off to Lake Chad to fish, she would be sent to her grandmother's to sleep. Other cousins were also there and they slept two or three, or even four, to a bed. Faithfully, at nine o'clock, her grandmother went around the house, making sure that the latches on the window frames were secure, certain that her little charges would soon be sound asleep. Once they heard her snore, they were up. Being the youngest and the lightest, she was the one who had to jump first from the windowsill, her shoulders serving as a pedestal for the others to climb down onto. The taxi driver, who was a friend of theirs, had been forewarned never to beep his horn, just to wait until they came out. Impromptu dances happened in the out rooms of bars or in beer gardens and the driver always knew the venue to look for. Normally he drove the elderly to church, but driving young girls was his reward. He had eyes for each one of them. He was a widower and used to say to each one, 'Maybe one of you need boyfriend,' and they would laugh and pretend not to understand. They were skittish, sharing the one lipstick, changing into shoes, as he drove along dark rutted roads, believing that from afar they could hear the voice of the disc jockey, the Romeo in his silver bolero, with his stack of records, calling, calling especially to them. 'Hurry, hurry, hurry.'

> Show me the diamonds
> Show me the gold
> Call me the answer
> Oh yeah
> I don't have a care
> This is my world

The dance place seemed like heaven. No matter that it was just in a field, boards slung down and soaked with some oil or other, and one kerosene lamp under which a boy sat with a plastic bowl, taking the money. In one place there were a few streamers, leftovers from an election two years previous. All the soppy trappings of love had their beginnings in one of those places and where the light did not reach, they would find themselves swept up in strangers' arms, hearing untoward things.

The driver sat at the back, making the one beer they had bought him last for the evening. He drank slowly. He basked in it. The smoochy songs, the beaming faces, the answering bodies and above all, the anticipation of the thrill that would be his when he brought them home. As he lifted each girl from the road over the fence and then from the garden over the windowsill itself, he was allowed a quick peck. She went five times in all.

Talking to the devil, talking to the Lord,
Going to heaven, going to hell.

Abruptly, her gaiety swerved into something else, something manic. She is like a dervish. I see sudden terror. A darker memory has claimed her – the pit, the horses, her father's face, the unending sadness of never being able to say goodbye. I hold her. I tell her it is going to be alright. She can live with us. I paint a picture of my father and mother in our doorway with tears in their eyes, about to receive us, brimful of welcome. My brother Yusuf in his blue shirt and striped braces is just a few paces behind, with a shy, tentative look. The worst of the dark is behind us. The tarred road cannot be too far away. The tar will be blue and soft underfoot, the same colour as Yusuf's eyes, a lapis blue in its depths, and soft with feeling. I called out to him, *Yusuf. Yusuf.* He answered with the bearing of a bridegroom. Then he vanished.

BUKI AND I STOOD outside the hut, quiet, downcast. We were snappy with one another. The sun was already up, sizzling on the plateau beneath and leaves drooped in the heat. There was nothing, no one. God has deserted us. I held Babby. Buki held Babby. You can't soothe a hungry child in a hungry place. Buki gave her something. It was the softest part of the root that she had dug up. Babby chewed it and spat it out with disgust.

'Cry. Cry. Cry. Cry your guts out. There's no one here. There's no one home. There's no mother. Mothers all dead.'

'Don't, Maryam . . . Don't,' Buki said in a voice so reprimanding. I bit back tears, ashamed. What had happened to the girl I once was. She was gone. There was no love left in me. I wanted to die. *I want to die*, I whisper. I did not know what I was saying. I did not know that death could be so near, that it hovered.

'I'll go forage . . .' Buki said as she went out. I did not answer.

I don't remember much of the day, except that it passed and Babby cried and cried herself to sleep a few times, rubbing her eyes that were scalding and itchy.

It was evening time again and we were at the table, about to eat. Buki had brought water and an orange-yellow fruit that she peeled and cut up in pieces. The flesh clung to the oval of the stone and she saved it, to make a syrup with.

It happened so suddenly. The malice of the morning had come back. This food was manna to us. We were starving and yet we had not touched it. Instead we were having an argument as to what it was called. She said one thing and I said another. We both got so headstrong and het up that neither would yield. Because whoever yielded would have conceded power. But what power had we, cast out in some hinterland. Vengeances flew.

'You do not love your child enough, you scream at her,' she said suddenly.

'You're jealous,' I replied.

'It's you who are jealous . . . and it's you who converted,' she said spitefully.

'I did not convert, nor did he ever compel me to,' I said. She resented him because he had separated us and she would never understand that he had joined the Sect to save his family from starvation.

'He saved our lives,' I screamed, so loud that even Babby cowered.

Then Buki did the cruellest thing. She picked up the bowl with the pieces of cut fruit, went to the door and tossed the contents out into the pitch-black night.

'I hope you're satisfied,' she said and went out.

*

I am hungry. My saliva thickens and drools. I want to go out and find where she has thrown it, to wipe the earth off it and bring it back and eat it. Why shouldn't I. I am ravenous. There is dirt on me and in me, the dirt of their deeds.

She is taking her time to come back, to show her mastery. *Buki, Buki. We are nearer than any two people and also further. Why don't you come in and bury the hatchet.* My mind runs between feast and vomit. Oh the pity of it. *You are the only one I loved, along with my mother and father and my brother Yusuf. The last I saw of my mother was her handing me clean underwear before I left to set out on that bus, to take my exams. I had had my first menses but it had finished. When they burst into our dormitory we did not know who they were, but very soon we did. We had heard of them and their brute ways, but until you know something you do not know it. They had burnt and looted villages and slaughtered the innocents in Borno, in Gwoza, in Maiduguri, but we had been saved, or so we thought. I had a clean wrapper. I had my diary. It was a little notebook. These entries would one day be our witness, or so I used to think. Buki, we are each other's lifeline. Come back in. I do not want this ghastly suspense. Night is so fearful.*

*

She comes in like an apparition, her hair wet, holding some root for us to eat.

'I got this,' she said, but barely were the words out than threads and spools of vomit were spilling from her mouth. Little black bubbles appeared on her lips. Her eyes were full of tears. Then she laughed, a hideous laugh and fell back. I see her black leg in front of me and I know at once. A stump getting blacker and blacker, like the rotted post in the garden. It weighed heavy. I fetched the blanket so that she could rest on it, but she is too feverish. She is struggling for words. Then I see the two cavities of red on her ankle, where the snake had bitten and where the venom had gone in.

'You're not dying,' I said as if the words could heal her.

She sat up, half smiling and lucid, then looked at me with the tenderest look and said, 'They are calling . . . they are calling me.' I knew what she meant. I had heard it once in my father's house, when his mother came to us, towards her end. They named it the death rattle and so it was, a sound beyond speech.

*

Under the moon, she looked so peaceful, like an effigy, her eyes closed and Babby next to her on the ground, weirdly quiet. I was digging as if she was telling me how to do it. There was no time for mourning. It had to be done promptly. I had chosen a spot a bit away from the hut. The earth was crumbling at first and I was reeling off the foods we would one day plant – spinach, onions, sorghum, rice, millet, nuts, Irish potatoes, gum Arabic. Halfway down I feel a ridge of stone under the spade and I scrape and scrape determinedly, but it will not shift. *Buki, I am not able to dig deeper.* I put leaves around her waist, as was the custom of long ago and I looked for the last time on her dark, golden, emaciated body. Then I lift her and lay her in. The grave is not deep enough. She is sitting half up, like a floppy clown. I did not cry. Neither did I fool myself that that grave would go unpillaged. I shovelled more clay over it and patted it and then I gathered some big stones, by way of protecting it. I had not said a single prayer. Then I picked Babby up and dreaded going back into that empty hut. I think she dreaded it also, because she kept pointing to where the stones were, so ugly and plaintive in a heap, under a ripe moon.

*

She bawled ceaselessly, drinking in my despair, my helplessness. The clay walls began to reverberate with her cries. I bring her outside. I sit on the chair and trace the ground with a bit of stick, begging for deliverance. I cry out, to Buki, to God, to the saints that I used to pray to as a girl, especially the little flower garlanded with pink rosebuds that fell onto her chest bone. June was her month. I wonder what month it is. I give her the breast, but there is nothing there. Then the answer came to me. Before my very eyes, identical to when we first saw it, lake water shimmered in the sun. I pick her up and go out. I am chatty. I will never know what I said on that walk and I will never want to know.

*

The old words were back that we learnt at the Feast of Pentecost. I had brought the basket. Up at the far end of the lake, away from the long-legged birds, there was a cascade of water that ran down from the springs in the hills above. The music it made! It would draw anything to it, even a basket. I placed her in it. The words were on my tongue – '*When the mother of Moses could no longer hide her child, she took for it an ark of bulrushes and daubed it with slime and with pitch and put the child therein and she laid it in the flags by the river bank.*'

Babby was in the basket, her hands dabbling the water at either side. I talked to her as I walked backwards. I talked so she could hear me. Big evergreen boughs jutted halfway across the lake and had embedded themselves there. They were good cover. They got between me and her. The moment I was up on the bank I scooted.

*

The mute spell of darkness had fallen but it was not mute in that hut. It was bedlam. I heard things. I stuffed the holes of the wall with leaves, certain that enemies were lurking. I put the stick to the door. It wobbled. I wedged it so that it no longer shifted. Then I saw her, in a wide pink bonnet, just sitting there on the ground. I tried to put a blanket around her but she refused to be contained. I had something to tell her, a revelation: *I have given you a name. I have called you Maryam. Same name as me. Two Maryams, like the mother of Jesus, except we are the Black Madonnas. We are descended from trees, they are our mother flesh. There are ebony icons that represent us. We are associated with miracles. That is why you and I are here. We have been in bondage, imprisoned in slime and mortar and made to do all kinds of hard service in the fields and elsewhere. Why are you looking at me like that? I am not crazy. Our black skins glow. Our heads are haloed. Don't go to sleep. Don't. I want you to hear me out to the very end. I want you to acknowledge your new name, Maryam, and to give me a little smile. That's better. We will be out of here by morning, on our way. Black Madonnas with diadems of gold.*

She had fallen fast asleep. I could not wake her. I lifted her, blanket and all, onto the bed, but I kept up the charade. Talking, talking. Somewhere, during that unruly night, I fell into a ravelled sleep.

*

Through the cracks in the door I see women's feet. There are three of them. One carries firewood, the second has a gaily painted calabash on her head and the third is holding my child. My child. She is wrapped in a clean blue cloth and is making sounds of contentment. The woman hands her to me as though it is a gift. I want to explain. I want to tell them how well she slept all night, not a whimper. They know this can't be true. They saw. They saw everything, the basket wending its way towards the cascade of water. They must have been gathering firewood at the very same moment.

I invite them in and the woman takes the calabash from her head and sets it down. She gives me a drink. I begin to take slow sips, but the vessel is shaking in my hand. They do not judge me. I think they guess that I have escaped captivity because of my mad, startled appearance. One of them speaks a little English. She has a big smile and when she smiles, I see friendly gaps between her teeth. I am not afraid of her. She tells me they are a nomadic people, but have a settlement some distance away. They are wood gatherers and they come in groups, so as to feel safer. Their men are away herding. They have been gone now for many days. It is like that, herders having to go greater distances each time, as the forest itself is being stripped of water and pasture.

There is nowhere for them to sit, so we go outside and sit on the ground. We touch each other's hands to compare how cold we are and to establish friendship. The woman lays small laths of wood over the dead ash from the fires that Buki made. She has a lighter. She uses it so adroitly. She wishes me to have it. Sparks sputter up into the grey blankety dawn and we sit without conversing. There is something exceedingly calm and safe about them and they are reticent, because of the crime they know I have committed. It is very cold.

Babby has come awake and is again mesmerised by red and violet sheets of flame, but still nervous of it. I take her to feed, but she is not hungry. How much does she remember. How soon after I ran did they find her. Seconds, even less. They see that I am sad and the woman tries to reassure me, says they will come with milk next day, because I must get stronger before I set out. But where can I set out to. I ask if trucks go by, because the previous night I heard sounds of vehicles. I tell them I watched over her. They look at me and see that I am lost. The woman who speaks for all says that it is not good for the baby and me to be alone here, but first they must take the advice of their men.

'We will try,' she says and I know that she wishes she could say it with certainty.

Then they leave.

Alone with Babby, I kiss her. Her eyes are full of something I call reproach.

'I'm not old enough to be your mother,' I say cravenly. Her expression is blank, aloof, her finger pointing into the distance with a kind of questioning thrust. I begin to cry. I cry from the pit of my belly. I cry from wherever the root of my love for her should be. She had never seen me cry so openly. She drops her finger and buries her head in my chest, the thumping of my heart the only sanctuary she has.

*

I have barely come out of sleep when I see the fidgety beams of a torch on the wall. Two men, wild men, in fur-trimmed hats and wadded jackets, stand above me. They carry a long pole, stretching from one shoulder to the far shoulder of the other, with animals tied to it. Hares, rabbits, a monkey with a grinning look and one big animal, its hind legs jutting out and black hairs sprouting from its hooves. It is an antelope. I saw one once in a picture. They are talking rapidly to one another in their own tongue. The torchlight twitching on the mud walls is making Babby quiver. Have they come to kill us? At least we will die together.

Then they lay the pole on the floor and look around hoping for food, except there is none. The younger one sat on the bed and the other on the broken chair. The young one took out a cloth full of eggs. He cracks them on the tin plate and they swallow them and grunt with satisfaction. Then I am offered one and I take it, being so afraid of them. It is a big egg and a very big bird must have laid it. The yolk is almost too much for my swallow and I retch, but get it down somehow.

The young one wants his reward. His eyes are dancing in his head. The older one goes out lugging the pole, the animals bobbing ridiculously on it. The young one begins to touch my hair and make loops and ringlets with his little finger. I know what he wants. Better to get it over. I put Babby on the floor next to the wall, as her basket is no longer there. I open my wrapper. The moment he sees my body, so raked and scabby, he draws back, gapes one more time and runs from there, shouting, '*Kola kola kola*,' which I know to mean *Crazy crazy crazy*.

*

The women returned very early the next morning as they had promised. When I told them what had happened they looked at each other and conferred and then the one who spoke English said I must come with them. It took only moments to leave, as our belongings were so few. Babby yelled for a wooden spoon that she had grown attached to and one of the women went back to get it.

BUTTERFLIES SCUDDING ABOUT, some across my face, others alighting on the stumps of horse dung on the ground. Two of the women had to hoist me by the elbows, up the steep hill towards the settlement. We had to sit a few times on the journey. It was a great distance, first through forest and then more open bush, with the sun boiling down on us. We avoided the villages.

Droves of children came running down in excitement, the littler ones almost naked, except for their thin vests. Mothers followed with still more children. At the very summit, I was put to sit on a stone. The floor was sandy and the beehive huts with their straw roofs and bamboo posts were the same sunny colour. An old woman came and sat by me. Her face contorted with pain as she kept gesturing, in order for me to know she had a toothache. Then a younger woman, possibly her daughter, appeared from one of the huts with two small bowls of milk, one for me and one for Babby. It was lukewarm and oversweet. The woman who rescued me told me that *Madara* was the name for milk and in my mind I called her that. I drank small sips, because I did not want to seem ungrateful. Babby was given hers from the thin lip of a calabash spoon.

She was then carried around to be introduced to everybody. A few hens scraped uselessly in the sand and the elderly kept looking around vacantly.

Hordes of children surrounded me, still unsure of my presence. A little girl, who wore a glass earring, touched me, then scuttled off in terror. Within seconds she was back, her hands on my toes, pinching them hard.

I asked the Madara woman what was wrong and she said the little girl was afraid of me.

'She thinks you are maybe a witch,' she said smiling and the little girl, who guessed that we were saying something concerning her, stood with her hand on her hip, trying to decide what punishment she might next inflict on me. The whites of her eyes had the mildness of milk, but the pupils were darting and plotting.

I was certain that I was about to faint again. The three women brought me inside, the door so low that they had to stoop to edge in. The hut was cool and as they laid me down on a narrow bed, with a white mosquito net above it, I thought it the kindest moment I had lived in a long time. On a big dresser there were painted enamel pots with shiny lids. Small strips of red carpet were thrown over a sagging sofa. I guessed that this was the woman's kitchen and also her bedroom and that she was about to give it up to me. She felt my forehead, then my pulse, and conferred with the others. She said I had fever and maybe a little bit of malaria, but that I must not worry. They had many remedies to make me better.

First I was brought to a washhouse and stood in a basin of water. Pails of water were poured over me. It was ice cold and made my teeth rattle. I was mortified at being naked, the fungus and mange of the forest upon me and my legs roped together in shame.

Back in the room, they gave me medicines. First it was a brown liquid that was viscous and tasted bitter. Then pink powders, which I had to swallow one at a time with a sip of water in between. They painted a paste all over my body. The three of them did it, with deft strokes and almost at once it began to harden. Then they wrapped me in cloths, layer upon layer, so that I was covered to my chin, and stiff like a mummy. I tried to talk, but I couldn't.

'You will have terrifying dreams . . . you will be sucked into them . . . but you will come back,' my Madara said.

She told me not to be afraid because all the impurities would be drawn out, the fever would subside. She gave me a cowbell to ring, in case I got too frightened.

They tiptoed out.

My dreams, as she foresaw, were grotesque. I could see the militants, every single one of them, changing shape and size, mutating into creatures, half man, half beast. Third eyes spooled from their foreheads, their grins were lipless and their different beards floated on a thin, bloodied soup. I knew that in my dreams, these encounters, awful though they were, had to be lived out in order to exorcise them. I am running, running, but they have surrounded me and I am caught. Then one breaks loose from them and whispers in my ear, 'I friend you.' He squashes me into an empty gas cylinder and follows, so that he can 'friend' me, except there is no bottom to it and I crawl out onto upturned earth, alive with insects. A little girl pops up. She might be me, or she might be the little girl who followed me, half fascinated, half mischievous. She is gabbling away – 'I left my hoe at the farm. I wish to have my ears pierced.' 'But your ears are pierced,' I say and I remind her of the long glass earring that she is wearing. Then another voice interjects, 'He did not declare his HIV status,' and I think it must be one of the girls up at the swamp. I see again the butterflies, landing as they did, on the khaki-coloured nuggets of fresh horse dung, with warm steam rising up from it. Something gauze-like flitted across my throat. Perhaps it is one of the butterflies that I saw as they carried me up. Everything I have known and seen and lived is pushing its way into those dreams and there are moments when I want to ring the cowbell, but pride stops me. The dream goes on and on. I see a sign on a door that swings back and forth in the forest and reads 'No Admittance'. Then I see my parents in the church and I run to them. They draw back from me, appalled, and are turned to stone. 'What crime have I committed,' I am asking, shouting, and brought awake by my own intemperate screaming. My Madara is by my bed, her hand on my forehead so reassuring. I ask her how long it has been.

'A long time,' she answers.

I am seeing with new eyes – the dresser full of painted pots with their shining lids. She lifts one lid to show me something. Inside it is a second pot that fits snugly into its appointed space and then more pots and still more, a family of pots contained within their primal mother. The cloths wrapped around me are wringing wet and so is my hair and she says it is a good sign, it means the potions have worked.

Babby is carried in to be placed in my arms, but she is more interested in the mosquito net than in me. Soon she is doing her goo-goo gurgles, her fingers agitating to be brought back out.

*

There is a certain place for me to sit. It is on a rock covered with a mat. A feathery weed of tenderest green separates the dwellings from the field beyond that is dotted with dark bushes and tall trees that stand alone. Every tree in its own slumberous empire. I am no longer afraid. There is so much activity around. Women sweeping and weaving, others washing clothes and wringing them out, still others carrying buckets of water up from the river. Many of the younger women are in the small gardens digging and hoeing. Without their gardens they would have nothing to vary their diets. But milk, as she says, is the mainstay of their lives; their cattle are everything to them. According to myth, their world was created from one huge drop of milk. Doondari, their God, came down from heaven and created stone, which led to iron, and then to fire, and fire created water, and water created air, and so the five elements were made for man to be created.

As herders they had difficulties. They were not wanted in the forest. They had friction with farmers who often insisted that the cattle destroyed their crops. It led to feuds and even to blows. Some of their young men, wild and passionate and so used to a nomadic way of life, sometimes lost their tempers and a young boy on impulse took a knife to a farmer, and harmed him. Luckily he was not killed. It resulted in the elders having to go to the court in the city, where they were not welcome and as a result had to pay enormous fines, which they could not easily afford. They had to sell some of their goats and also some sheep, because there was a saying among them – 'If you kill my cow I kill you.'

Since then, the government were less willing to issue the permits for their certificates of occupancy. As she was telling me I felt ashamed at being a burden on them, but I was unable to say it. I could see that the cattle, the ones who had not gone with the herds, did not have much milk and also they needed spare milk to barter in the village for grain, dried fish, sugar and sometimes medicine.

The children are no longer pestering me. They play, and by her cries Babby yearns to be included. Their toys are all of clay and mostly dolls. They poke these figures with thin sticks, to make eyes and ears and nose and mouth. The boys look across and shrug. The boys have their own game. They run old tyres down the hill and have races at rolling them up. The little girl who feared me hangs around. Her mother tells her to stop staring and to bring me a flower. She runs off and comes back with the tiniest sprig of blossom, drops it on the ground and is gone again. The moment I pick it up the petals shed. Her mother says she is only ten, but already betrothed to a boy from a tribe in another village. She will marry in three or four years and they will obtain a piece of land and move away and start their own herd. They will not move too far away, because it is essential that they all keep together.

Someone whom I imagine to be their chief is being helped out from one of the larger huts. He walks on two sticks and is led across towards me. He is a tall man, a scion of tall men, and in his eyes, weak though they were, I see an unquenched pride. I want to thank him for allowing me to be there, except he has already launched into a recitation, which a young boy translates, as he knows it by heart. Before he sits, the old man points with one or other of his sticks to hallowed spots on the surrounding hills:

> That is where my father is buried.
> That is where my grandfather is buried.
> That is where my great-grandfather is buried.
> That is where all my ancestors live.
> We will never give up this way of life.

Once the old man has sat down, the young boy, with vaunting pride, recounts a summary of their history. It is for my benefit:

We are nomads from North Africa and sub-Sahara. We had resided since the fifth century in these lands, the curse of Oba Egbeka was upon us but with God's instrument, we prevailed. We prevailed against Hausa kings who were not following the teaching of the Prophet. They were imperfect Muslims. We launched a Jihad in 1804, under the banner of Usman dan Fodio.

*

My Madara and I have grown closer. I knew how busy she was and yet she made time, so that I would not be lonely. It was by the river, just the two of us and the sound from the river so happy and musical as it purled along until it had to clamber over a set of rocks, where it tumbled and left a foam of lace behind it. Bits of that foam followed down into the water with the lightness of feather and these feathers grouped into little islands of idleness.

For a while we were silent and yet I knew, or rather I guessed, that there was something she wanted to say to me. Even her voice was different, more confiding:

He was the tallest man I had ever seen. He stood inches above my father. The blue of his head cloth was a regal blue. He and my father were in deep discussion. Somehow I guessed that it was about me. I was mending and patching at the time, under the trees where I always went to do my needlework. He had not seen me, since it was forbidden, and yet he must have sighted me somewhere.

Afterwards, my father came alone to talk to me and I said, 'I like that man,' and my father asked did I mean yes and I answered, 'YES,' with an eagerness. My mother was also happy. It was time I married. She bought two new wrappers at the market and a bracelet made of coral beads. On the following evening, the head man from my future husband's settlement came with three white heifers, in return for my hand.

The following morning I left home. Young girls walked me halfway until we met girls who had been sent to escort me. Everyone shook hands and parted. I never fully saw my husband's face until I was alone with him. He delighted in every aspect of me. Earlier, an older woman, who had dressed my hair, told me that his previous wife had died young of fever, as there was no way of getting her to the hospital in time. They did not have transport and they did not have stretchers. He mourned her for the best part of a year.

The young men were not permitted to see me at first, but as soon as I was noticeably pregnant, I was allowed outside. Women schooled me about many things, taught me the necessity of patience and good temper. My children would be my life, just as for the men their riches were in their herd. I had four children in a short space of time, the last being Shehu, your little tormentor.

But passion wanes, and when after a period a husband sees a beautiful young girl, who will bear beautiful children, he goes to her father to seek her as a wife. It is how it is. If I had said or done bad things, bad things would have resulted. If I had shown jealousy, I would have been punished for it. The elders would have told him to stop coming to me. If I had persisted with these bitter humours, I might have been sent back to my parents and that would be the most damning punishment of all.

Then very earnestly, and so that I would remember it, she said, *I am happy wherever I am set down. I have my place on this beautiful earth, as everybody has.*

*

Word came that the cattle and the men would be home by evening. A boy in torn clothes came running up the hill and no sooner had he spoken than he lay down, exhausted, his mission done. His teeth were very white and the grey-black slit on his face became sharply defined under the sun. It was a mark that every boy and every girl was given at the youngest age. It was done with a razor, then covered in charcoal which is what gave it a darkish hue. Some deemed it a mark of valour, and others a mark of beauty, saying every incision was different.

*

I heard the cattle long before I saw them. It was a sort of thudding, the rapid clomping of the hooves on ground as they moved across the vast plains. Then they came into view, hundreds of them, a ravishing patchwork of colour, white and brown and mottled, blending together in one flowing, moving mass. They had boomboxes around their necks and the music, even at a distance, was blaring and shrill. Their great horns forked towards the heavens, as if they were inscribing their homecoming to the sky. The excitement at the camp was infectious, everybody busying and Shehu running in different directions, willing the cattle and the men to hurry on. Somewhere, she had acquired a slide for her hair.

All day the preparations were hectic. There were pots of soup, simmering. They had been made from peppers and onions, with different leaves for flavouring. In the dairy, women were busy making cheese balls, a speciality which they knew the men loved. The older women were washed and given clean head ties. Young women took turns braiding each other's hair and teasing one another. They let me sit among them. We could not communicate, and yet I was happy, content. Although I wanted to go home to my mother and our house, I was reluctant to leave. The place and the peaceful way of life had made me tranquil.

We lost the herd for a time when they had come on a valley that was flooded, and though they revolted at having to swim, they were made to do it, and boys who could not swim clung to the forking horns for dear life. Amidst a great hysteria with shouting and moaning and music they reappeared and were driven in a gallop across the road. They baulked at the trench – the same trench that I had been carried over – but then close to home, they cantered up the hill, boys chasing and coaxing them and calling them by their names that were identical to children's names. The few that strayed had to be chastised and brought back and one dug her front legs into the ground, refusing to budge. Two boys got her up, then thwacked her, scolding her all the way, until they reached the hilltop where all the older men had come out to look at them and welcome them home. So carefully did they study them, feeling their bones and their bodies for thinness and making various enquiries of the herders. Then there was the ritual of milking. Certain cows were taken out from the group and the men milked them into ornamental calabashes, which the women took and ritually carried up the hill.

The men were fed first in a hut while the women waited outside. Then the women ate, and afterwards the men came out and sat on the ground, but as yet there was hardly any conversation among them. Soon boys began to tell of their adventures and everyone listened intently. I could not understand the stories, but from their movements, with raised fists and jowl to jowl, I guessed it was about scrapes and tussles they had encountered in the six weeks they had been away.

Then a young boy who had been guarding the herd in the

pens came in, holding something in his hands, and everyone went quiet. It was a newborn calf. There was jubilation. The youngest child was presented with it and her mother had to help her to hold it as the little calf trembled so much. The old men gathered around.

The shy messenger who had brought the news earlier in the day took a pipe from between folds of cloth and came forward to play. The notes, so soft and timorous it drew sweetness out of the grassy slopes all around and the cattle in the pens began to moan softly.

Once he had finished, he withdrew into the shadows, but the men were already jumping up, their arms swinging and the women answering with deep, avid chortles. Then they stole under the men's arms and faced them, inviting them to dance. Two drummers had already settled themselves on stools and the music, so stirring, sent a summons across the valley, even to the revered places where the ancestors lay. Everybody danced. Children rubbed the sleep out of their eyes and sought out their mothers so that they could dance with them. The reserve I had seen earlier between men and women had gone. This was how they met. This was their way of expressing themselves to one another.

Then a young girl whom I had not seen before came running in. She wore a red wrapper and big metal hoops hung from her ears, her nostrils, her ankles and from her snake-thin braids. She was from the next village and had heard the cattle come home. The women welcomed her and shook hands with her. Once she got her breath back, she joined the dance. She swirled and moved from group to group, like a girl in a trance and yet she did not seem to acknowledge any one of them. She danced for the dance itself. Her effect on them was so stunning that gradually they drew back and began to watch. Even the flute player came out of the shadows to admire her. He couldn't not. The talkative young men went on their knees, moving nearer and nearer to her. They teased the shy man and dared him to dance opposite her. They kept goading him, pushing him in her direction, and finally, gathering his courage, he stood up and said, 'I like your dancing.' My Madara translated it for me. The girl did not respond but she had heard it.

That was how things started, just by their seeing one another. Always that distance, that in its depths sought nearness.

I thought, I am awake but dreaming. I am dreaming this boy and this girl who have just met, yet with an unspoken pact between them. I dreamed them, because I knew I could not ever dream anything like that happening for myself.

*

I was sitting on the bed when my Madara came in. There was something wrong. Her big smile was not there. I thought that maybe she had had a quarrel with one of the men. It was the formality in her voice that made my heart lurch, but it did not occur to me that it was about me. Why was she so cold, so aloof. She did not sit down. She spoke standing and her voice was firm. 'When the women went to the village this morning, the vendors at first refused to speak or do business with them. Word had got out that we were hiding a militant's wife and child. Everyone down there is in terror. They know what will happen. Their goods will be confiscated, their stalls burned down and they themselves slaughtered. Then the Jihadis will come here for us, they know how to find us, they know every inch of this forest. They will destroy everything. They will take our herd. There will be nothing left of us.'

'I will go,' I said half rising, wanting to thank her for the endless kindnesses, but she rebutted it.

'My son will take you both, before it is light. He has gone to the village to borrow a cycle,' she said, as she moved away from me.

Close to breaking, she turned and said, 'We hate to send anyone away . . . especially children,' then made her way under the carpeted curtain that served as a doorway.

THE PLACE WAS DEATHLY SILENT, surrounded by trees, the building itself completely disguised with leaves that were themselves squeezed into wire mesh. Some of the older brown leaves stuck out and it was that crinkly sound that I then heard.

The boy on the cycle had dropped us a distance away and sped for his life.

I recognised it was the military post, because of the sandbags piled around it and wires jutting from the roof. Men are shouting at me. There are two of them in baggy military attire, hoisting their guns. One fires into the air, so that the birds fly out in frenzy. There is the sudden flapping of wings, birds not knowing what direction to take and the lower branches swirling violently. The hush of dawn is broken. The second one takes phones from his pockets, and untangles the various cords.

'Drop her . . . drop her,' is being yelled at me. I put Babby on the sandy earth, where she lies, silent and stricken. Never had she looked so forlorn, an abandoned parcel that could be kicked or trodden in an instant. She screams when they run the metal rod over her and goes into convulsions. I am not allowed to lift her up.

'Take your belt off . . . Take it off,' one says, and I realise that they think I have come on a mission to blow them up. They assume I am a suicide bomber, I am one of the little girls that I had seen under the tamarind tree, eating the dates that she had just been given, and childishly excited because of being promised Paradise.

'I have no belt . . . I have no weapon . . . I just want to go home,' I said.

'She just wants to go home,' one said with a snigger. He tells me to undress.

'Shake them . . . shake them,' I am told and after I have done it, I have to undress her then, as the metal rod has to be trained over both our bodies. She jumps as if she is being electrocuted.

One fires questions and the other records everything on his telephone:

'What is your name?'

'Who sent you?'

'Who is the person who brought you on the cycle?'

'Why did he leave so fast?'

'Name your father.'

'Name your mother.'

'Name the elders in your village.'

'Why don't you remember?'

'If you lie you know what will happen to you.'

I answer as best I can, but I know that they are trying to catch me out. Then they hurry towards the building, to report on my arrival, change their minds and retrace, as once again the rod is trained over us and over the harmless pieces of clothing on the ground.

They hate me. I can tell by the way they look at me. All they want is to find a way to prove that I am guilty, arrest me on the spot and have me sent to a barracks, then a place of death.

A third man, a commander in a more elaborate uniform, comes down the steps. Ridiculously, they stand and give him the formal salute. He is tall and gangly. He does not seem so het up as his subordinates. I tell him that I have no belt and that I have no button to press and that I am not here to blow anyone up. He takes it in, then asks how can he believe me.

'How can I believe you?' he says for the second time.

'I would rather blow myself up than blow other people . . .' I answer. He looks at me, stares into my eyes, to see if I am lying. He turns to the others and says that it is more likely I am one of *the schoolgirls*. It shows in the eyes, the trauma in the sockets of the eyes and the hunted look. He has seen it before.

'What age are you?' I tell him that I don't know.

'High-profile,' he says, irked now that this whole business is going to take time, a lot of time, exceptional circumstances and so forth. He looks on the phone, where he can read the questions they have put to me and the answers I have haltingly given. Then he takes long strides back into the building.

Left alone with them, one goes to where my clothes lie on the ground and undoes the knot at the corner of my wrapper, having noticed where money was hidden. It was the money Mahmoud gave me. I had kept it throughout. It was to be our gift to my parents when Buki and I got home. She strengthened that knot many times. He pockets the money, knowing that I won't report him, that I daren't.

The tall man returns and gives the order to take me inside. Without deferring to any one of them, I pick up my wrapper, partially cover myself, then pick up Babby and tuck her shawl around her – a petrified parcel.

The room is small and stifling hot. Guns stacked against the wall and weapons piled everywhere. He takes a cylinder with a long snout and pointing to a trip wire, says if I had stepped on that, I would not now be availing myself of his hospitality. There is a table with a brick under one of the legs to keep it from wobbling and a calendar with a cellophane window showing the exact date. He sees me look at it, mesmerised. A time, a day, a season.

He sat me at the table and told me to write a report so that it can be conveyed to HQ, who are already getting hot under the collar.

I write of our capture, the work we were made to do, the cooking, the cleaning, the prayers, the regular beatings, but I do not include the savageries in the Blue House. I say I was married, gave birth and how, along with Buki, we escaped when the government bombarded the settlement. I describe girls dead on the ground, and others left behind with every hope of theirs extinguished. I tell of the hut and the fire that Buki made and how she was bitten by a snake and died. He reads it over my shoulder while I write.

'How do you know it was a snake bite?'

'She told me . . . she had gone out in the dark to forage and when she was pulling up a root, she felt the bite . . . I saw the bright red marks of its fangs.'

'Ah, the venomous creatures,' he says and from a shelf above the table, he fetched a manual. With it, another book fell, that was titled *Great Expectations*. It had a picture of a dirt floor with men in caps and overalls and hens pecking in a black-smith's forge. He reads aloud – '*Snake bite advice – Dos and Don'ts . . . Facts and Myths*.' Then quickly, he tosses it aside.

Once again he is suspicious, muttering, 'something rotten in the state of Denmark' and so forth. What if I am not telling the truth. What if I have left something out, something portentous. He says I am a puzzle, nay an enigma. I have walked through an immense forest, rife with dangers, landmines, hunters, different militia, thirst, hunger, and yet I arrive at this military post, albeit in shock, but in one piece. There must be some mystery.

'The herders found me . . . They saved me,' I tell him. He ponders it and after some time seems to believe me.

'What is going to happen to me?' I ask. He can't say. The big brass in the city are now studying my case, X saying one thing, Y saying another. Stasis. Obfuscation. Disagreement. I might be moved on to a more up-to-date military base, his little unit being so rudimentary. He apologises if the buffoons have been heavy-handed, but I must realise that to them I am not a girl, I am not even a person, I am the portent of death, I am a decoy, sent to create a distraction before an attack.

He sat on the stool next to me, saying there was something I must know. Human nature had turned diabolical. The country as I had left it was no more, houses torched while people slept inside them, farmers no longer able to till their land, people fleeing from one hungry wasteland to another, devastation. A woman pouring her own faeces on her head and her children's heads each morning, to deceive the Dogs, to delude them into believing they were all mad.

'Only a few days previous, a woman arrived at the post with a dead infant, claiming she could not bury it without first killing a goat. Could I find her a goat. Could I kill it. No burial was complete without this. Hopelessly, she lay down on the path where you stood, and after she had cried her fill, she got up and went on, bewailing her predicament.'

One of the buffoons rushes in, to say the satellite is down.

'Fix it . . . Get it back up,' he shouts, and seeing that I have cowered, he apologises and asks if I am thirsty. With alacrity, he pours water from a jerrycan into a tin mug, with flaps at the side that serve as a shaky handle.

'You find me unhinged,' he said then, and launched into a spiel of his life:

'I go home every six weeks or so and I am a stranger to my family. They sneer behind my back. My daughter says I must see a therapist, so morose am I. We argue. I refuse to see a therapist, I hurry back here to this cradle of evil, I see the buffoons take turns with the hammock I had specially built for my injured leg. I have come, you might say, for the last act. Same trees, same darkness, same looming uncertainty. Why am I telling you this . . . Because I do not know you, and, moreover, you do not know me and you do not know the world you have come back to.'

From the table drawer he takes a newspaper cutting and reads the most recent statistics – 'In this country up to two million people have fled their homes, 1.9 million people are currently displaced, 5.2 million people are without food and an estimated 450,000 children under five are suffering from severe malnutrition.'

While he was talking, Babby was tetchy, and tugging at me to be fed. He saw how embarrassed I was and got up, hitting at the table wireless and looking outside to see if there had been any developments. It took time to feed her as she was unsettled in this rowdy place and kept losing the nipple. I was still holding her when he came back in. He just stared at us, not uttering a single word until she had finished. Then I burped her, and gradually she drifted off into a doze.

'How do you feel?' he asked me.

'I am good, thanks.'

'You are good, thanks,' he exclaimed in disbelief. What was it, this symbiosis of mother and child. He had to admit that watching me, it awakened something in him, something good, an attachment maybe or a sunset or the beautiful cadences of Charles Dickens. He gets carried away in praise of mothers. Barefoot, supplicant, living on scraps and yet carrying on, carrying on. They do not cut their throats. They do not cut their children's throats and drink the blood. They bear it, just as they have borne their children. He asks how they do it, these mothers with children, how do they do it, how do you do it. His face was within inches of mine, his eyes so questing.

'Make me feel,' he said.

'Don't send me back to them,' I said.

It shook him. He looked abashed. He picked up a cardboard box with MOD printed on it, lifted the lid and plonked it on my lap. There were fruit bars, biscuits, energy drinks, dried meats and cheeses. From the selection he pulled out a bag of toffees, handed me one and then helped himself. We sat there, chewing our toffees like two errant children. When he had finished, he folded the piece of paper into the shape of an aeroplane and sent it skiving out in search of news from beyond. I read the lettering on the box – *Twenty-four-hour Multi-climate Ration Pack*. He asked was it not ironic that the grub no longer deemed worthy for an English garrison was sold to him and his cohorts. Likewise, the soon to be defunct weapons. He got carried away. He cited history. The colonisers come for the spoils, the gold and the ivory, mocking the quaint customs, the witch doctors, the witch dances, the rainmakers, the cannibals, yet quietly becoming attached to the place. He reckoned that certain English drawing rooms would be full of charming memorabilia, swords, knives, cutlasses, maps, and old photographs of men and their ladies lounging on terraces at sundown. He even ventured that in the basements of various museums, there would be severed heads, pickled in salt, that had once been a feature and openly displayed in glass cases.

One of the buffoons came rushing in to say that a top general wished to speak with him, at once.

I was told to go outside. It was getting light, the sun had risen as it had indeed each morning, but never ventured down into our cursed enclave. I hold her tight, tighter. I talk to her. I wonder where we will lay our heads this night.

The buffoon who had stolen the money from my wrapper came and stood very close to me, and smelt me as if I was a dog. It was his way of telling me that the money also smelt. His way of silencing me.

From then on it was a question of being sent in and out, listening to them speaking on their phones but unable to guess if there had been any developments. The commander was more brusque, telling me to go back inside as it seems the satellite worked better out of doors.

It may have been the heat or dread or tiredness, but I have

fallen asleep on the stool and am dreaming. I know that I am dreaming:

I am crossing a field with Buki and Babby. We each have her by the hand. She must be older, because she has learned to walk. We are scared. There are shapes behind the trees and hidden in the bushes. We have to get past them and also past a big house that is a madhouse. I know it is a madhouse but I don't know how I know. It has small windows that are barred. In the layers of hedging all around, rats are trying to scramble out. Rats and their young. We can hear them nibbling at the wire and squealing as their tongues are cut. We shift towards the middle of the field, where there are mounds. Buki has gone, disappeared. I walk with Babby and hold her so that she doesn't trip. Then there is a strange and marvellous occurrence. A panel of earth begins to move slowly towards her, then completely effaces her chest, shielding her all the way down to her ankles, a sort of armour. We walk on, regaled. In the distance there is a house. It is lit up.

I waken with a jolt. The commander has returned, saying as yet there is no definite decision, except that he seems more hopeful.

He decides to buoy us up with a moment from Charles Dickens and his voice, as he reads, grows mellower.

'I was in England again – in London, and walking along Piccadilly with little Pip – when a servant came running after me to ask would I step back to a lady in a carriage who wished to

speak to me. It was a little pony carriage, which the lady was driving, and the lady and I looked sadly enough on one another. "I am greatly changed I know, but I thought you would like to shake hands with Estella too, Pip. Lift up that pretty little child and let me kiss it!" (She supposed the child, I think, to be my child.) I was very glad afterwards to have had the interview; for, in her face, and in her voice, and in her touch, she gave me the assurance that suffering had been stronger than Miss Havisham's teaching and had given her a heart to understand what my heart used to be.'

Someone had entered and when I turned and looked I saw it was a policewoman, with her navy cap peaked at a jaunty angle.

'We are taking you to the city,' she said as she helped me and Babby up.

I forget the walk down the path, I forget everything except for being inside a big car, the leather seats smelling of wax. There were two other cars, one in front and one behind.

The policewoman had to wind the window down because the commander wished to say one last thing:

'It was all . . . all . . . quite . . . miraculous,' he said. Then with a flourish we are waved on. He looked forlorn.

The buffoons stood to attention, their chests puffed out at having fulfilled their duties.

THE CITY IS TEEMING with life. Cars, motorcycles and taxis all edging their way in and out, the taxis no bigger than perambulators. Passengers are squeezed into them, their belongings on their laps. Babby is sound asleep in my arms, despite all the jangle.

Sun beats down on stark white buildings, their black gates ablaze with spears of gold. Watchmen sit under the shade of the trees, chatting with policemen who stroll around. Other policemen stand in narrow white booths, directing traffic and stopping cars. Our car is waved on, because of a military flag attached to the side of the bonnet.

The policewoman pointed to what seemed a mountain, but was in fact a rock, a rock so famous that its picture featured on the currency notes. She spoke of its fabled history and the many assaults attached to it. Water ran down its sides into the innumerable veins, like endless tears of lamentation.

The trees are not as ample as the ones I cowered under in the forest. Younger trees bordered the lanes of the motorways, their leaves wrapped around their trunks, like folded umbrellas.

In between the stately villas are shacks made of assorted things – cardboard, wattles, bamboo, and here and there a panel of zinc roofing rasps in the sunlight. Women are stooped over their small cooking fires, with hordes of children needing to be fed. On cement walls, painted signs for fridge repairs, motor repairs and one in jet black that read *Call Mr Chef*, with a phone number beside it. On a huge hoarding in coloured letters I see the edict *Become a Millionaire*. Underneath it, someone had scrawled *Cotton is the Creation of God*.

At a busy intersection where four roads met, two young boys without legs whizzed around on skateboards, their hands outstretched and when a coin was tossed, they raced each other to be first. Different youths tapped on the window whenever our car came to a standstill. They were holding up crayons, flip-flops, bottled water and little plastic bags of mixed nuts. The policewoman told me to ignore them.

We arrived at sets of double gates that led into parkland, where there were numerous buildings, also a glistening white, and long flights of steps up to the entrances. Various officials greeted us. Then a woman came forward and called me 'Pet. Pet.' She said that baby could do with a nappy and we were brought straight to the bathroom, which was an abode of marble and mirrors. Beside the washbasin was a tray to change her and she kicked with glee, her eyes roaming at the opulence of her new surroundings. I caught sight of myself in many mirrors and gasped at the alien creature I had become, my mouth full of sores and my hair in splices. Babby was almost toppling off that tray, but I caught her just in time and marched us around to gape at each other. She pointed to the two images in the mirrors, not know-ing who they were. The woman who called me Pet was rapping on the door, as doctors were waiting to examine the baby.

I am in a small consulting room, with the woman sitting opposite me, telling me how brave I am and how resilient. I am a survivor. She is trying to put me at my ease. She says I will have tests, injections, vaccinations, treatments of different kinds, but most of all, it will be a 'listening therapy'. They are there to be humane, to be supportive. She wore a plain, short-sleeved dress and leather sandals with shiny buckles. From the peepholes in the leather, I begin to see pink worms wriggling out. I cannot stop trembling. She asks if maybe I want to talk, but I don't. She takes a little calendar from her pocket and starts to calculate and add up the number of days I have been in captivity. The calendar has a picture of different saints for each month. She shows me her favourite – St Teresa, the Little Flower, a girl with fine features, and for a necklace, a garland of pink rosebuds. Then she opens the page on St Patrick, an imposing man brandishing his crozier. St Patrick, the patron saint of Ireland, who, in the year AD 432, banished all snakes, human and reptile, from her country. She went on to say would that he might be resurrected, he might put a stop to the carnage and abominations that were happening all around.

'How old am I?' I ask.

'Oh, you poor child . . . you're hurting . . . you're hurt-ing,' she says. Then from inside her dress she takes a brown cloth scapular, kisses it and tells me it is mine. I feel the hidden engraving of some saint's face, tucked into the cloth.

'Hold that when they're cutting you . . . but they'll be kind enough,' she says as an afterthought.

At that very moment the door is pushed in and two men in white are wheeling a trolley. They put a gown over me that ties at the back. They have white masks over their mouths. I think they are messengers from heaven.

The woman walks beside me as I am being wheeled along the corridor. She is holding my hand, squeezing it, uttering – '*Lord have mercy, Christ have mercy, Lord have mercy.*' Endlessly.

'IF YOU SMILED, you would be far prettier,' he said. If I smiled! He is the doctor assigned to bring me back, he says it take fourteen days for the human mind to readjust.

He will have seen from the various notes on his desk, written by others, that I am withdrawn, that I am sometimes listless and that I am given to irrational bouts of anger. He will also know that I tore up the veil they gave me. It was the glowering blue that the Dogs had dressed us in. He knows that I am afraid to cross the road and that twice I have refused the offer of a walk in the park with a nurse.

'You are no longer in that forest,' he says.

'You weren't there,' I say hastily, too hastily.

I am shackled to it. It lives inside me. It is what I dream at night, with a baffled Babby slung across my belly, imbibing my terrors.

Daylight comes at last. Fruits cut up in wedges for our breakfast. She picks out a piece of melon or papaya, studies it and then plonks it in her mouth. A little glutton in a pink high chair.

I want to scream at this man in his dark suit and his jellyish eyes behind thick curved lenses. Not once has he touched the water in a little plastic cup set down before him. I drink mine and stare into space. If only he had an instrument or a wand that he could put inside my head then everything would be revealed and there would be no need for these hesitations. He asks if I like my room. Have I remembered to take my medicines. Is my child's health improving. To each and every question I nod *yes*.

'I should have kept the placenta,' I say abruptly.

'Why should you have kept the placenta?'

'They ate it . . . she could hide in it if we are ever separated.'

'You won't be.'

'But how do you know?'

He sees the fear welling up in me and pauses.

*

I tell him things, in order not to tell him things:

I sieved corn and prayed. The chaff blew about and the wind hurled it into the hard desert dust. I cut up rumps and saddles and bush meat, flies and worms swarming on them. John-John swatted the flies with a cricket bat and I decapitated the worms with my sharp knife. They wriggled even when dead. John-John found the cricket bat in an abandoned camp, where he also found a book on the rules of cricket. I did not pray hard enough. Rebeka prayed and she escaped.

'Who is Rebeka?' he asks.

'Maybe she died,' I answer.

Then I tell him about Norah, a little girl who was helping her aunt to mind the flock and lost contact with them. She was about ten years old. They got scattered. She was running around calling, calling when she was captured in the hills. The soldier who caught her was smitten with her. He took her as his. She said she was too young. He said, *You have relatives, you have an aunt, I can go after them.* She used to come up to the swamp, blood running down her legs, calling, calling. *Dawo, dawo, dawo.* Come back . . . come back . . . come back.

He knows there is more to be said but that I cannot tell it. Between us there is this yawning chasm.

'When is my mother coming?' I ask, brusquely.

'All is under consideration,' he says.

I think how my mother is waiting every hour for the summons to come and bring me home. Just as I too wait.

*

I am in talkative mood telling him of the Black Day. Twelve girls were told to wash and cover themselves nicely. They were given porridge before setting out. There was going to be a swap. Twelve girls would be released for fifteen of their fighters who were in prisons in the city. Those of us who were left behind felt wronged and embittered.

They arrived back in the dormitory in the middle of the night, broken and deranged, too shattered to talk. They were without headdresses. Either the thorn trees had torn them off or they pulled them off themselves in an act of defiance. They lay on the floor and howled. We made a circle around them. We were all together then.

Over the days and the weeks we learned what happened although the story differed with the time and they had become so muddled that they contradicted each other. This much we knew. They had walked over fifteen kilometres in roasting heat. They arrived at a small clearing that had been recently cut and young grass sprouted from it. The plane was already there, a small white plane with the propellers rusted. The old trees that had been felled lay around like sleeping animals. From inside the plane they could hear singing and shouting. The prisoners were impatient to be let out, to go down those steps to where their brothers waited and kiss the forest that they called home.

People from both sides were meeting and dispersing, sometimes friendly, sometimes not. Most of them took shelter in their trucks and those in charge of the paperwork sat under huge umbrellas. There was a tall man in a white kaftan, acting as mediator.

The girls were not offered even a drink of water. Although faint, they believed that soon they would be going up those narrow steps into that plane, where they would be welcomed and buckled into a seat and maybe offered a nice cool drink and a welcome.

Many hours went by.

There were small differences between the two sides and sometimes harsh words were exchanged. Then there was shouting and cursing and vengeances were vowed and clods of earth were thrown at the plane itself.

Then they knew that something had gone very wrong. The man in the white kaftan threw his arms up and in several languages said he had wasted a year of his life on these negotiations. They knew for certain when an officer who had been inside the plane, obviously guarding the prisoners, stood on the top step holding an open suitcase, brandishing it and shouting at the Jihadis on the ground. He had been guaranteed a sum of money, which was not forthcoming. He waved it frantically. It was old and battered and the lining was ripped. Everything became uglier and more threatening. They laughed, relishing their hatred, each side certain of the future annihilation of the other.

The mediator had gone. The plane door was shut. The trucks were moving away and the girls were ordered to turn around and walk the fifteen kilometres back.

I could not go on. I reached for one of the paper tissues in the box that I had never dared to touch.

He said nothing, did nothing, just listened as I described the girls still there, clinging to the belief that one day they would walk towards that clearing, the new grass, the small white plane with its propellers turning for lift-off.

I cannot believe that I am actually confessing to my nightly slaughter. It gets gorier with each night's dream. I am boiling my captors, in big black pots. Many fires are lit. These men know their time is up. They beg for mercy the way we begged. I pile them into the pots and John-John is assisting me with the pounder. We smash their skulls and their brains ooze out in a kind of murky mush. Their beards float on the surface like rotting scum. The boiling water rises up around them so that they are silenced. They have to eat of themselves, their eyes craved with crying, except they cannot cry, being dead.

Girls are running free from the dormitory, throwing off their vestures of shame. They wash in the rivers. They smell clean. They smell of nature again. They eat mushrooms. They bind their hair with juniper twigs. Word has gone on ahead. From the villages, families have set out, bringing dates and singing the old songs.

He removes his glasses, wipes them thoughtfully and looks at me.

'One day, you will open your heart to someone,' he says and rises.

It was our last session together. We had broken the ice.

AT FIRST SIGHT of each other, my mother and I gasped, a gasp that only we could comprehend. Too much had happened. She had changed beyond recognition, torn by sorrows. She looked older, and her eyes were bleary. It was in the hall of a government building and she was out of breath from the last climb of steps. People were guiding us, making sure that we did not feel too intimidated in such grand surroundings.

Judith, the young American nurse who had seen me a few times, rushed in, her hair all tangled, so as to give me a gift. It was a rubber ball that I could squeeze whenever I felt the heebie-jeebies coming back.

'Squash the bastards . . . Squash the bastards,' she said, cupping the ball between the palms of my hands.

Mama and I were allowed a few moments alone in a reception room. It had to be quick because the President was flying back from somewhere, especially to greet us.

The room we were led into was very large, with a long table and chairs down the length of either side. There was a flask of coffee on a tray, along with cups, saucers and a packet of biscuits.

'Don't ask me anything,' I said.

'I won't,' she said.

It was there that she broke it to me that my father was dead. From the moment I was captured, my father was never the same. He went up and down roads saying my name. He built a wooden seat under forked trees that looked out onto three adjoining roads so that he could see me coming. He said my name when he talked in his sleep. That was how she realised he was dead. He was no longer repeating my name. His heart gave out. I wondered why she was so distant and why she had not embraced me. I put it down to the strange surroundings. I thought in a little while, we would be sitting somewhere quiet and less ostentatious, spilling our hearts out.

Moreover, the guard who stood outside the entrance door, and whose shadow I could see through the top half of the panelling, was tapping on the glass to say our time was up.

There was a host of cousins waiting for us, some that I remembered and some that I did not. They were all dressed up but one seemed to be the ringleader, ordering the others where to stand, et cetera. She was introduced to me as Auntie, but she was not my aunt. I barely remembered her. She was the most famous cousin we had. We went to her house very seldom because we were poorer. She had married an army officer who got promoted to general and then moved away. It was said that he left her but they were still officially married. In her house the walls were crammed with photographs of the general in his army uniform and his medals and sometimes Auntie yoked to him in one of her shiny dresses and looped necklaces. There were also families of dolls on window ledges, with their legs spread out. China dolls with painted cheeks and pigskin boots.

A nurse followed soon after with Babby in her arms and I sensed a certain chill as they recoiled. Not one of them rushed forward to admire her.

'She has the same little frown in the centre of her forehead as you,' I said to Mama, and they all looked at me with revulsion.

Auntie began to explain to me that the government did not approve of bush wives bringing back their children, but instead found crèches for them to live in. I felt so hurt at being called a bush wife, and not by my name. She said that in my case an exception had been made because she pulled strings. She made sure that the baby would be brought back to our own village. Mama told me to thank her. She was beaming with pride. Auntie said they would leave that afternoon as the city was far too jangly and far too unhealthy for a sick child. I knew I was being deceived but I was unable to challenge them. The last I saw was Babby being held by a nurse, swaddled in a clean white shawl, the crown of her head concealed in it. She had a green soother in her mouth, with a row of beads dangling from it so that she could suck and play with the beads at the same time. She did not fret at being separated from me. She was enthralled by her new surroundings, staring, pointing at things, then gazing up at the lit chandeliers that poured pools of light onto the marbled floor and picked up chinks of colour in maroon and pink and ochre.

IT WAS A FEVERISH DAY. Crowds. Speeches. And veneration.

I had been given a new purple dress with a purple lining to hide the ghastly gore within and also a matching veil. Mama had a flowered dress with wisps of gold that hung from the seams and trembled when she moved. Her hair was perfectly braided, in a salon where they also bathed her feet in a basin of whirling water. She was still cold with me, and far friendlier to those around her who were praising her courage and her faith.

An aide kept reminding me to smile, so I smiled. She had also briefed me on what to say and what to withhold. People did not wish to hear gruesome stories. 'Nothing negative . . . nothing negative,' she kept whispering in my ear.

We were driven to the President's residence early so as to avoid the crowds and any intrusion from press or cameras. When we got there we were led directly to our seats. A carpet of the same intricate design led from the hallway into the reception room, where the flags of the neighbouring states were furled on poles, inside the bay of the window. Pink curtains were drawn to shut out the glare of the sun. Chairs were placed on either side of the central aisle and different chairs at the very top in a semicircle where the President and his entourage would sit. They were covered in a peach-coloured satin and there was not a stain on them. Everything was perfect, the chalk-white mouldings of the ceiling, the shining wooden columns, the exact folding of the curtains and yet it felt cheerless. I smelt flowers but there were none. I reckoned that the room had been sprayed earlier to give a semblance of nature. We sat stiffly. I could hear Mama's gigantic sighs. Maybe her dress was too tight. An urge overcame me to slip away to wherever Babby was. I felt she needed me.

Mothers who had been invited were arriving in batches, the dust of their journey on their feet and on their ragged clothing. They recognised me at once. Their eyes settled on me and I saw those craven expressions, all reaching for news of their own. How could I tell them the truth, that some girls had died in childbirth, others in different bombardments, some sent to more remote camps, and most bafflingly of all, some had chosen to stay in the camp, where they were thankful to have at least one meal a day.

Nothing negative . . . nothing negative . . . was spinning through my mind.

There was a fanfare as the President and his entourage were announced. It was a cavalcade of government ministers, their aides and military men with badges and medals emblazoned on their chests. The ministers wore richly embroidered hulas, and the President himself, the tallest among them, wore a chaste white one with a wide gold band. He was like a man in a sphere of his own. The women were too afraid to clap loudly and almost too afraid to breathe. Instead, they craned forward to be that bit nearer to him. A woman in a blue dress took her time to sit comfortably and then gathered the folds of silk around her ankles coquettishly, all the time smiling.

The President wore a half-smile of accomplishment and slight disdain.

The first to speak was a governor from a nearby state. He veered from joy to grief, mopping his face with a large spotted handkerchief. He said he spoke for the entire nation when he welcomed me home, calling me a beacon for all, saying that an emotional tsunami swept the country once the news was announced. Then, with an unctuousness, he thanked the President, who had cancelled a trip that very morning to be with his own people. This was not a president flying around in jets, or skulking in state rooms, this was a president who cared for all entrusted to his leadership. Every child mattered to them. He cited the millions of naira allocated for school fees, for the feeding of students in public schools, for books and pencils, transport and all the other necessities that are a growing child's birthright. To the mothers hoping he might have a magic wand, instead he had to ask for patience, forbearance, but in his heart, he believed the national catastrophe would soon end.

'Our country will hold its head high again,' he said, and again dabbing his forehead, tears welling up in his eyes, he said unashamedly, 'If I had not had a Western education, I would still be herding goats.' The crowd loved it, they clapped unrestrainedly. Then, gathering his composure, he pointed to the President and said, 'When you have the real, you scorn the shadow,' and the President stood up to speak.

The President was more incisive and damning – 'Visibility. Candour. Power.' Each utterance of his was like an arrow. The audience knew they were in the presence of greatness, of the man who held the key to their shorn lives and the little piece of ground they subsisted on. He looked around, saw their apprehension and in a more humorous voice said, 'We shall dare our enemies to a warring duet.' His cohorts smiled at the human touch.

Then, he spoke of his determination to bring the reign of terror to a halt, reminding them that it could not happen in the twinkling of an eye but with cunning, know-how and strategy. Then, barely consulting his notes, he spoke fluently and with passion – 'I ask you to dispel all doubt, conjecture and fictive reporting. We are fighting this war. Our enemies are everywhere. They seek martyrdom but they are not martyrs. How shall I name them. Hyenas. Yes, hyenas. You not only have the known fighters, but you have others in association with them, exploiting the unrest, operating under their rubric. They are waging a war against us, against our institutions and our rule of law. They are intolerant of everyone and of everything. Just think of the numbers they have taken down, policemen, prison warders, civil servants, leaders, schoolteachers and innocent children. They are against Christian and Muslim. They detest religious pluralism. They are rapacious. But make no mistake, we are winning, we have seized back territory and swathes of land that they have stolen. Our top military brass is equal to any country in the world, even the United States. A vast amount of our national budget is spent fighting this war. We are upgrading weapons and machinery to wipe them out and they know it. We will not accept canards as truth. We will stymie their actions in every way. We will disarm them. We will impotise them. We will wipe them out. We have taken cognisance of their glaring acts, of their pathology of lying and killing, of their infection in our body politic, but we are at the helm. They will disappear. They will burn in the crucible of our might. They will be the hunting dogs that failed to obey the whistle of the master.'

When he stopped talking there was a hushed silence. The fact that they had been within reach of him had given them something, a sprig of hope. But I wanted to speak, to say, *Sir, you are only a few feet away from me, but you are aeons from them in their cruel captivity. You have not been there. You cannot know what was done to us. You live by power and we by power- lessness.* I thought of my friends at that very moment, under the tamarind tree, some maimed from the bombardment, some newly pregnant, insects feeding feverishly on them, mouthing the same prescribed prayers. My aide guessed my agitation and was telling me to sit still and show good behaviour.

Having concluded, the President was moving slowly up the aisle, basking in the awed admiration, his underlings ahead of him, while the mothers, with tears in their eyes, clutched one another's hands, knowing they would never live so august a moment again in their lives.

The lady in blue was all smiles, citing my courage, my determination, my pluck, my poise. A wild forest was no place for a girl alone and yet I survived, I persisted, I came through. She made no mention of my incarceration and did not speak of Babby. She stretched out the hand of friendship and said that by returning I had given a seedling of hope to all the other mothers. She felt about me as if I were her very own daughter, who had been taken in the dead of night and miraculously restored at dawn. The people were so stirred by her sincerity, by her candour, that presently they were standing, surging towards her, chanting 'Mama, Mama,' and she thanking them effusively. They were her people, she prayed for them morning and night and apart from a fondness for a particular football team, they were her family, as were all the stranded mothers in remote villages, not having the means or the privilege to be in these rarefied surroundings.

Then, in a more muted voice, she asked for leniency. She knew how each one of them would like a time alone with me, but it was too soon and emotions were still raw. Would they be kind to me. Would they not deluge me with questions, because, despite my poise and my beautiful dress, I was fragile. Put simply, she said, they should think of me as someone taking baby steps back to life.

'We aim for a soft landing,' she said, still smiling, and gesturing to Mama she led us towards a marquee, saying it was time to party, to welcome a heroine home.

*

The music was deafening. People talking, eating, dancing. All their mad hopes squeezed into this one day. I moved aside, so as to be alone for a little while.

A tall girl in a white veil came towards me. The veil was decorated with gold crescents and yet she was like someone in mourning. She did not speak at first and then, when she did, it was in a sudden burst, as if she had not spoken to anyone in a long time. Not until she said my name did I recognise her. It was Rebeka, who had jumped that first evening, as the truck lurched its way around a belt of trees.

'I prayed . . . I asked of God if these were bad men . . . to please help us to escape. God answered for me. I whispered to you to jump with me.'

It was as if we both relived the same moment, the truck slowing down, other trucks behind and Rebeka standing up to grip an overhanging branch, then risking the jump, thinking that I was following, because she had entreated me so earnestly. I heard her fall with a soft thud because of the ground being so loamy. She went on to describe herself lying there, alone, certain that the trucks would follow, and see her white blouse very clearly under the bright moon. Except they didn't. When they had all passed, she stood, but found she could barely walk. She hid in the upper branches of some of the trees and stayed there until the first sight of dawn.

She was certain as she walked along that she would see the smoke from the school, except she didn't, because it was too far away. She met a farmer, who asked if she was one of the captured 'schoolgirls', then fled in terror when she said that she was. Further along she met another man who was dragging firewood in a cart, pulling the shafts of the cart with a rope, and seeing her stumble, he took pity on her, even though he guessed who she was. She sat on that pile of wood until they came within sight of a village and then she was told to get down. He said to keep to the tracks no matter how indistinct they became, because much of the undergrowth was mined.

The smoke from the school had almost died down, but the smell hovered in the air. The grounds were covered in a layer of grey-white ash, with charred books and burnt satchels. The place was mayhem, children with mothers, parents demanding news and teachers being castigated for not having done more to protect the innocent girls.

A woman brought her a pan of water to wash her feet in. Her parents, she was told, would arrive the next day. So overwhelmed were they that none of them could speak. They wept, they just wept and clung to one another. They wept in the bus going home and when it got to be known that she was the girl who escaped, there was impromptu applause.

At the welcoming party a few days later, people had pooled together to buy food and gifts. She was given combs for her hair. Yet, within weeks, trouble started.

Infidels . . . Infidels was daubed on walls and everyone knew the significance of it. Someone had informed. The Jihadis would come, not just for her, but for her whole family and the entire village. She had to leave. It was with deep emotion she stressed to me how her family had prayed and mourned. They assured her of the depth of their love and gave her apples for the journey. She was packed in a lorry with sacks of corn, squeezed into one of those hemp sacks, almost smothered, as the lorry had to go across country, on a far longer journey, in order not to be seen.

In the city an American woman, who ran a charity organisation, took her in and helped her to rebuild. She encouraged her to read and to write out the words she did not understand. She was given a series of English stories that concerned the dippy adventures of a dog, and though it was a nice story it was not for her, it did not touch her heart.

After six months she had to move, and she lived now in a hostel with ten other displaced girls. Luckily, she had found work. She took care of the altars in several churches, waxing the furniture, washing the linen and arranging the few flowers that were donated. It was this, perhaps, that made me think at first that she had joined some religious order.

All of a sudden, she was shaking, and asked if we could go and sit somewhere quieter.

'I will never forgive myself,' she said, quietly, and I could see the shame she carried at having left us.

'I have sickness,' she said, whispered it.

'What sickness?'

'The Jihadis will take me. They have powers over me.'

'They don't. They can't.' She was trembling so badly she had to hold on to a pillar. She refuses a drink of water.

'I want to be normal,' she says, the voice urgent.

'You are normal,' I say, although I too am jangled.

'Maybe we can meet up,' she said and for the first time, she smiled.

'I am going home, Rebeka.' I blurted it out, I had to.

'They will reject you . . . They will turn you out,' her voice ugly and spiteful.

'I have a baby,' I said, thinking it wiser to tell her.

'A baby!' She was aghast. It was all she wanted. A baby of her own, its heartbeat next to hers, a little companion through life.

Suddenly she announces that she must leave.

I saw her hurry, alone, a fugitive, in and out between the crowds, the sun picking up the glints of gold on her veil. She could not get away from that firmament of power quick enough. I had shattered her one hope.

I THINK IT STRANGE WHEN my mother announces that we will sit by the swimming pool, she who had been so distant with me. For our last thirty-six hours we had been given a room in a grand hotel. It was twenty-nine storeys high.

It is evening time.

We find a table in a quiet corner, as there is a garrulous party in full swing. Balloons are being hoisted up and float randomly about. Gourds of liquidy light dip from the trees and baby lights are magically roosting in the greenery. Yet despite this beautiful setting, my mother is surly.

She had said that she wanted to talk. First it would be about my father and then, no doubt, it would be about my captivity. I am uneasy. Waiters in smart uniforms are darting about with trays full of drinks, moving so swiftly, yet never once crashing into one another. Frogs are mating and one of the revellers is recording the croaking sound, for the amusement of others.

'Animals. Butchers,' she says and looks at me as if I should already know, then says, 'My men are gone.' She blurted it out. I knew that my father had died and now she is telling me that Yusuf is gone.

'Dead?' I say, but I cannot believe it. A black void is rushing through me at the thought of going home to a house without father or brother.

'All they could bring me was his good blue shirt,' she says and in her ravelled thinking, she is still clutching that shirt as if they have just handed it to her.

I try to ask her a question but she is incoherent, talking rapidly, jumping back and forth in time, consumed by spectres.

The Jas Boys started to come around after dark to talk to Yusuf, to induce him to make a pact with them. They knew how much he missed me. They had seen the drawing he made of me, which was hung in the church porch. I could be got out at a price. There were ways of doing it. Other girls had been whisked away from that very same secret location. It is where our soldiers or vigilantes never went, deeming it too dangerous. The ransom money was astronomical and sums had to be paid each month. All this she learned later from the men who had found him and buried him. He had quit his studies and taken a job with three haulage companies, bringing livestock and maize to different cities. In those self-same cities, he was able to give blood many times, on account of being a stranger. He earned money whatever way he could. She found a hoard in an old bath out in the yard, and took it to mean he was planning to leave.

'Everything was set for a night in October.'

'Which October?' I ask. I have to know.

'Which October!' She is rasping now, telling me I am devoid of feeling, even as I am seeing that isolated field and my butchered brother.

'You don't see . . . Not the way I see,' she is saying. I stretch my hand across the table. She does not want my hand. This is her grief, hers alone. She has become a sort of fiend, tearing the extensions off the crown of her head, flinging them in a hard and hating way as if they are dead rats.

People look across, wondering if they should intervene.

'Talk to me, Mama . . .' I plead with her.

She becomes sad for a moment, recalling the quiet of the evening, waiting in her kitchen, the Bible in her hand, which, although she could not read it, gave her fortitude. Yusuf had returned after being gone for three days. His dinner was warming between two tin plates. He looked exhausted and distracted. He went down to his room and came back quickly in his best blue shirt, saying he was meeting with a manager about another job, with better pay. Then he walked out. That was the last she heard of him, until men came knocking on her door after midnight.

Words flew out of her like lava, re-enacting Yusuf's death, Yusuf's hacked death, and it was not as though she had been told it by two workmen, but as if she was now the medium on whom it fell, the onus of revenge.

Yusuf was gone and I remained. She is blaming me. If I had not been my father's pet, if I had not insisted on a secondary education, if I had not taken that bus, none of this would have befallen them. The *if*s of accusation hung in the air like the dying cries of the mating frogs. I wanted to make up. I was home, or almost. I put my hand out yet again to reach her, but she tore further with her braids like some crazed goddess, flung them around as if they were evil.

People began to stare across.

'We should go upstairs,' I said.

'You are ashamed of me,' she said.

Then a drunk man came towards us, trying very hard to walk in a dignified way. He offered us a drink but my mother declined. He said the setting was too beautiful for dishar-mony, he remarked on the lights, mimicked the mating frogs and scolded me for having disobeyed my mother. Mothers, he insisted, were the backbone of the country. His friends came and dragged him away and they all staggered off.

The silence was deathly.

'Babby will bring us back together,' I said after some time. It was the last straw. Her face had turned to stone, her mouth twisted. I thought of the stone fonts in the churches with the small crevice to dip one's finger in. I cannot dip my finger into my mother's heart, evermore.

Everything inside me is breaking up. I want to hurt her and wipe her face in each grotesque and horrifying thing done to me. I fear her. I hate her. Except I no longer know what hate is, or fear, or love. I have a baby, I miss her. I want her heartbeat next to mine. My brother Yusuf will not be there to greet us when we get home.

Mama gets up and walks with her head down, watching her every step, as if she is afraid she might fall.

The lights wink out one by one.

In that solitary atmosphere the balloons float, limp, unclaimed and clueless.

MY LAST SIGHT OF THE city was of our hotel building, which seemed to be toppling. Down below in the street, a begging woman is bent over, sweeping up the debris with a broom of withered palm. We are going home, Mama and me.

Further along, under a canopy of trees, money-changers in long white kaftans swarmed on us as our car slowed down in heavy traffic. Their rake-thin arms were thrust through the window, clamouring to do business. Our driver dismissed them, but they persisted, brandishing wads of notes, each one insisting he would give us the best rate, all of them repulsed at the sound of the horn, which the driver hooted repeatedly.

'I keep you safe . . . I bring you to your homes safe,' he said. He was very proud of his big car and told us that the government had had it specially built in Canada and fitted out with the most up-to-date equipment.

The fanfare of the previous days swam before my eyes – the swelter, the speeches, the blaring music and Rebeka, wraith-like.

There were two other passengers in the car, one of them a man with a dirty scarf wrapped around his face and his eyes half shut. His name was Esau. The second man, who was

English and who sat in front next to the driver, turned to us and said he had paid for two seats, because of his ungainly long legs. He said it in order to be friendly. He and the driver had struck up an immediate conversation, and Esau, feeling left out, leant forward to overhear.

'Tell them, Esau . . . tell our companions what happened to you,' the driver urged him. Esau was halting at first, but nevertheless eager to tell it and I felt he had told it many times:

I lost territory. I lost Binta. I lost everything. The Jas Boys didn't impact on us, so we thought we were safe. Then one evening they came. I was putting the doves into their cotes, as Binta and I kept lovebirds. I heard shooting. People screaming and running and I ran like all the others. Binta was not back. She had gone to market to sell some of her pots. After a week or so some were lucky to be reunited, in the bush, in church halls, in dry wells and in caves on the mountains that skirted the forest, but not us.

He is overcome with emotion, describing the clay pots Binta made, pots to keep water cool and littler pots to store palm oil and butter. How they were prized. People gave them as gifts. Their colours were a deep earthen brown, but also fired with the magic blends of Binta's imagination. If only, as he said, he had grabbed one pot as he ran, he would now have something of her to hold on to.

'We find her . . . we find her,' the driver said, but Esau was now crying unashamedly.

Once he had regained his composure, he told of a chance meeting with an aid worker who mentioned a partially blind woman named Binta, in a camp, who spent her time walking up and down the road, expecting her husband to come for her. According to the aid worker, she said she would recognise her husband's footsteps, on the very threshold of the underworld. With time, he made his way there and among the constellation of sad and broken faces, there was no one who resembled his wife. Much later on, he met a trader who told him a happy story that revived his hopes. It concerned a little lost girl, also in a camp, whom the trader met when he went there on business. The little girl had a telephone number written on a torn piece of paper that she believed was the number of her uncle, who had fled their community after the war began. The uncle had moved to the Plateau region, and they had heard that he worked as a mechanic in a garage there. That piece of paper was all she had between her and the abyss. She found it in her father's pocket after he and others were executed. She asked the trader, since he travelled around so much, if he might locate that uncle and see if they were blood relatives. It turned out that they were. She worked night and day, doing farm work near the camp and then one night, without telling the steward, she ran away. Her journey was mostly on foot, always hungry and always afraid. The uncle was stunned the day she walked into his garage to ask for help. He had a new wife and three children and it would not be easy to persuade his wife to have another mouth to feed. Nevertheless, they took her in. This the trader learnt months later, when he found her in dungarees, working as an assistant in that garage.

Fearing that things were getting morose, the Englishman volunteered to tell a story. When he left university, full of countless plans, he decided to come here briefly, do some fieldwork and perhaps write a thesis on his findings. Instead, he had stayed almost eight years, travelled all over and had many adventures. He slept in the Sahara under the stars – 'A star-spangled sky' as he termed it. There, according to local tradition, he learnt how his future could be revealed. When he saw a shooting star, he was to take a pinch of sand before the star disappeared, then tie the sand in a rag and sleep on it. Whatever pattern the sand had formed during sleep was a symbol of his future fortune, except that he had completely forgotten what the various configurations stood for.

Pointing to a long range of mountains in the distance, he told us then that he had lived with a tribe whose ancestors had settled there hundreds of years back. They knew nothing of life down below. They did not know who was in government or of the oil boom that had come and gone. If there was conflict, as there sometimes was, the elders in each family were called to settle it. They were completely self-sufficient. They grew corn in the little patches of field between the surrounding scarps and also built terraces for climbing vegetables. An unwieldy spreading shrub had been woven into a sort of rookery that not only protected them from the Sahara winds but was also a hatching ground for guinea fowl, bush fowl and once a year, a marvellous migration of lime-green butterflies.

Hausa cavalry, as he then told us, had their annual tournaments up there in the centuries gone by. Those feasts lasted for days and he had found records of them in old almanacs. Meats, game, poultry, palm wines were served and flowers, such as marigolds, taken between courses to help the digestion. The chefs were from Arabia and the cuisine so exquisite that the outer skin and feathers of peacocks were removed before cooking, then meticulously restored, to give a lifelike appearance. Acclaimed minstrels and storytellers were despatched from beyond the Red Sea and one of the fabulists was renowned for being able to speak through the night, to send sleepers into a trance.

Because of his having mastered the skills with the plough, the chief emir offered him the choice of one of his fourteen daughters in marriage. It so happened that he had never actually met any of the daughters or the wives. If he came on young girls in a group, sifting grain or cracking kola nuts to make butter, they hid their faces, went into peals of laughter and then clung to one another in mock terror, as if a pharaoh had come into their midst.

'So you weren't bewitched,' the driver said.

*

No sooner were we out of one city than we came on yet another and another, each one smaller and swarming with life. People walking, people cycling and old people, gaunt and hungry, sitting on the steps of a plinth that had been erected to some forgotten hero. The stalls were of cardboard, canvas and bits of umbrellas, their entrances crammed with goods of every kind. On the street, stacks of tyres covered in shiny white plastic. Squeezed in between these stalls were places of worship, signs that read *Jesus Lives* or *Christ Is Everywhere*. On the opposite side, signs and scrolls to Allah, alongside big posters of politicians with immaculate white teeth and similar posters of beaming preachers and their wives.

The road blocks got more rudimentary the further we went – barrels or sawn-off branches of trees just flung down. We came on a group of women who began to wave animatedly at us, as if we were old friends. The Englishman said it was a common sight, women taking it upon themselves to fill the potholes. They held up the stones as proof of their labour. They were laughing loudly. Some laughed so much I could see their teeth and the gaps between their teeth. In their eyes, curiosity and rampant hope. Who were we in this important car and where might we be going? They showed no resentment at the fact that we did not give them money, but were reinvigorated as they waved us on.

At the next sentry post we were not so lucky. A sullen young man shone his torch inside the car, with evident disdain. He asked to see our papers. My mother's hand was trembling as she hauled out a sheet, a handwritten inventory of her family going back many generations, the ink rusted with age. The sentry sneered and the driver reproved him for his insolence. Luckily the fracas ended with the driver, grudgingly, throwing a few naira onto the road and the car sped off.

Mama whispered to me that she wanted to ease herself and I whispered back: could she wait a little longer. I felt awkward asking.

'Look . . . look,' the Englishman said, pointing to a field of sorghum, the leaves green and wavy in the breeze and women kneeling in the furrows, picking out the beans that were trained up along the stalks of corn. I saw what was like a patchwork of green needles in islets of water, but I did not know what they were. The Englishman said it was a rice paddy, which farmers had only just begun cultivating in the past couple of years. It meant two harvests and less hunger.

Finally the driver pulled in by a petrol station and asked if the ladies might like the 'facilities'. To one side there was a small structure and in black paint the word *Mosque* had been written, except that some letters were swallowed in the grains of cement. There were three kettles by the entrance, kettles without lids and of different colours. There was also an inked sign which read *Male and Female* and an arrow, which we followed. We could see a man in the male closet, his head jutting above the side wall and he turned and scowled at us. The female closet had a door but it was locked. My mother was agitated. She asked me to keep watch for her. I could hear the quick splashes against a wall and immediately a colony of ants crawled out onto drier ground. My mother was calling me to help her.

As we walked back towards the car, I saw a girl not much older than me sitting on a litter of rags, talking furiously to herself. She was muttering and arguing and she used the rags to hit out at flies and onlookers. I wanted to give her something from our bag, but my mother pulled me away, saying she was one of the mad creatures. By nightfall she would be brought to a police station for a few hours, then let loose again, or else some man would drag her into the bush.

Just before it went pitch dark, on a lonely stretch of road, the Englishman asked the driver to 'Stop, stop.' It was very sudden. On the roadside, a little girl was holding a pan of oranges in one hand and in the other a boy, probably her brother. The Englishman got out and we could see him talking, then handing over some money, as she tumbled the oranges into a big kerchief. She kissed the ground after he got back into the car. With his penknife he began to peel the oranges. He was expert at it, so that the skin never broke. He had made entire twirls to mimic oranges. He halved them, took the pips out and divided them equally among us. It was such an unexpected moment of gaiety, us sucking and slurping, the juice dribbling down our chins, eating everything, including the white pith. There was general agreement that these were the sweetest oranges any of us had ever tasted.

Further on we came on the burnt villages, trembling shells of blackness, the bamboo stalks, on which the huts had once stood, charred and buckled and weird black fungus sprouting everywhere. The saddest of all were the gaping window holes, where people had once looked out at the passing world.

We were quiet for a time, each thinking our own thoughts and the car kept sliding in the potholes, loose stones flying up, as the driver suddenly decided to make up for lost time.

A ringing phone made us all jump and the Englishman suddenly realised that he was reaching his destination. He spoke softly, but the people at the other end were talking excitedly, interrupting one another and asking how much longer he would be. Then, quite formally, he shook hands with Mama, myself and the old man and gave us some boiled sweets to share. The car came to a screeching halt by a ruin and his friends were already there and coming forward to greet him. They embraced and soon we saw them go up a steep hill, their shadows colliding into one another in the sporadic light from the several torches.

We were sad to see him go.

*

Esau got out to sit in the front. Night was not far off. The trees looked darker and the spaces between them in purplish-black shadow. There was such bleakness and want and I thought of the shivering child selling the few oranges and kneeling on the ground in gratitude. No one on the roadside now, just one solitary figure walking towards the bush with a mattress over her head and a boy trying to round up a herd of white goats. I pictured Babby being handed over to me by the big-bosomed auntie, and the surprise running out of her eyes at seeing me again, but not kissing me, punishing me a little for having left her and finally, sucking on the collar of my blouse to claim me.

*

The mountain was at one with the sky, steaming with a black and violet vapour.

'The old North is dead and the old venerations are gone,' Esau said, his arm raised in homage as he spoke to it.

It was the story of a boy and a bull.

That boy was his grandfather, who had been specially selected and was made to train for three years. It was an ancient sacrifice that happened each year, to appease the god who slept in that mountain and was responsible for the harvests. If the god was left hungry, then the people would starve.

On the appointed day, the bull's feet were tied front and back and four youths took turns with the rope. The bull roared and rammed against man and rope. It did not want to go. It knew. It folded its legs going up that mountain and lay down, refusing to move.

Crowds of men followed and larger crowds, also men, had gathered up there all night, chanting and praying for the bull's plenitude. A fire had been going for twenty-four hours and the power of the blaze could be seen in neighbouring states all around.

All his grandfather carried was a small knife with a bone handle that fitted exactly into the groove of his palm. He was both afraid and exhilarated, man and bull within inches of one another, able to smell each other's fear. He knew, because he had been taught, that the first thrust was the defining one. Then the moment came. The crowd went suddenly silent. His grandfather, as he would later tell it, gripped the horn in one hand and with a skill he was not sure he had, plunged the knife straight into the main artery, so that blood came in one vast torrent and the bull roared its maddened lament. The god was appeased. All his grandfather could ever recall of that primal moment was blood everywhere and the howl from the bellies of the crowd. Others helped him to finish the bull off, but it fought and charged until there was no life left in it. Once the legs caved in and it lay helplessly, it was carted over and lifted onto the roaring fire, where juniper leaves had already been thrown. Every part of that bull got eaten, except for the entrails.

Esau remembered the knife that took pride of place in his grandfather's house and visitors always commented on the size of the blade, how small it was. He had been allowed to hold it over the years and often had gone in alone merely to touch it, to relive its history.

'We are almost there, ladies,' the driver said, turning. Esau had nodded off the moment he finished his story.

*

When we arrived at our own village there was not a single light. The driver helped us out and Mama apologised for the fact that we did not have a spare bedroom. He assured us that he and Esau would find a hotel on the way back.

'Plenty of hotels,' he said blithely, as if we had been driving through a succession of bustling cities. Then in confidence we learnt that whenever he could, he brought Esau along. Esau spent his life hanging around bus stations and taxi ranks, asking strangers if by any chance they had come across a partially blind and beautiful woman called Binta.

'Hope is better than no hope,' the driver said and Mama and he exchanged blessings.

Our kitchen smelt sad. Even in the dark I could feel an atmosphere of disorder and neglect. Mama groped then found the matches and lit the kerosene lamp. In the guttering light, I saw two things, Yusuf's blue shirt, the emblem of martyrdom, stretched along the wall, held down with brass tacks and a tall man emerging from the bedroom. I presumed it was my uncle. She had mentioned that he had come to our house after my father's death but she had not told me he was living there. He wore a baseball cap back to front and had pulled on a jacket over his night attire. He saw me, but he did not greet me.

'Did you eat anything?' were Mama's first words to him, but he did not answer.

'Where is Babby?' I asked looking around, because I had not heard a single murmur. Mama and he exchanged a look.

'Babby is with Auntie,' she told me.

'When is she coming?'

'Soon,' Mama answered brusquely.

She was fussing over my uncle, taking some eats from the gift basket we had been given, which she set down before him. There were bananas, little cucumbers and biscuits. Hardly had he sat down than he demanded salt.

'How soon?' I asked, determined not to be fobbed off. I could tell by their expressions, by their haltingness, that something was wrong.

'Go to bed,' my uncle shouted and so I went on down to my old room. I still had my little torch and saw that the room was a shrine of dust. Dust had adhered to every single surface. The scented sheet of paper was gone from the drawer and instead there were old clothes, rags and a pair of broken glasses that had been my father's. If my father were there now, this would not be happening.

I was crying when Mama came in.

'We do not have the power to change things,' she said as she set down the lamp on the little table by the bed.

'Why not?' I asked.

'Because we are women,' she answered. She was vexed with me.

She pretended to be too tired to discuss anything, undressed and got into bed face downwards. I stood over her. I had to know.

'The stigma . . . the stigma,' she finally said. I could tell it was a word she had picked up from him.

'What stigma?'

'Bad blood,' she said and I saw everything then, as an approaching nightmare.

'She's a child,' I said.

'She won't always be a child . . . she's tainted . . . she'll grow up to be one of them.'

I could not believe her words. I knelt by the bed and still she would not answer.

'What are they going to do to her?' I asked. I tilted her face and saw that her eyes were sick with terror.

'I have to know.' I was screaming it, I was berserk.

'He'll take the stick to you, Maryam . . . he'll take the stick to you,' she warned.

She managed to blow out the lamp and begged me not to incite trouble, not then. Maybe he had taken the stick to her too.

We lay there in darkness and confusion.

'What will happen?' I ask. All I need is a crumb of hope. She cannot give it.

'Only God knows the answer to that,' she said.

THE WELCOME HOME PARTY a week later was a fiasco. We had been loaned a barbecue. The air was thick with the smell of spices and the fat was sputtering everywhere.

Mama had already told me that Auntie was not coming, as Babby was chesty and they did not want to expose her to unnecessary infections. I both did and did not believe it. Even as they arrived, these cousins and neighbours, I felt a freak. I could read their minds, by their false smiles and their false gush. I could feel their hesitation and worse, their contempt. I knew they were thinking, *Jihadi wife, with the Sambisa filth still clinging to her.* Mama said that I was to sit with them and to thank everyone for coming. The smell from the roast made them holler their hunger, even though the smoke hurt their eyes. I was trying to remember each person's name. Obie, an old woman whom I used to gather firewood for, came and mashed my hand. I remembered how she used to read our futures in tea leaves. She was on the verge of tears. She knew what had happened, just as she knew things were not right between me and my family.

'Take ginger,' she whispered, as if it was my only hope.

Then a strange thing happened. A woman, unknown to

us, came marching into the yard, swinging her arms, her hair tied with different bits of ribbon and twine. There was something provocative about her. She asked for food and drink, demanded it, yet never touched it when it was set down before her. She kept looking at me, a steady look, saying that a spirit was telling her one guest was absent. I knew she meant Babby. She left without touching the food, which was considered ungrateful and when Uncle followed her outside, to see in which direction she went, she had vanished.

I felt someone touch my arm and turned to find Abigail, like a blaze of colour. We were friends at primary school and I used to help her with her lessons. Her braids, that were henna-coloured little serpents, piled high and roped around the top of her head. Their ends were tied with teeny metal balls that tinkled, and one glass bead dropped onto her forehead like a talisman. The whites of her eyes were big and soft, so clear and besotted. She wore a red wrapper with matching top and lipstick of a fuchsia colour. 'I am the fuchsia girl,' she said to the gaping women who looked on and the men who feigned indifference as they drank their beers, a distance away. She studied style and colour co-ordination in the pages of the magazines that her father brought back at weekends. He worked as a night porter in an embassy in the city.

The moment she saw my phone in its knitted case, she asked if she could look at it and then just gazed and gazed. Whereas I saw moons and bubbles, swimming in a haze of marcasite stars, she saw her man, her prince, smiling out at her and sending positive vibes.

'I am in love,' she whispered and steered me away, towards the kitchen, so that we would not be overheard. Then cradling the phone in the hollow of her neck and without dialling any number whatsoever, she spoke into it. She was thinking of him. 'All the time. All the time. It was not you who made me HIV positive, darling, because you would not do that to me. I feel nearer to you than I have ever felt. When we meet we will discuss everything.' She is assuring him that it was that stupid bitch in the hair salon, where she had her braids done, that infected her. The bitch had a gash on her finger and somehow their bloods got mixed, because the braiding took forever. In the clinic to which she went each week, they assured her that she would be cured. Then she half knelt and asked if I would allow her to phone him once a week and in that way she would feel connected. He always attended Friday prayers in some city or other, so that she would be certain to track him down. On other days he was travelling, because as a skilled carpenter and joiner he was needed in different cities.

'I have a baby,' I whispered.

'I know,' she whispered back.

She knew, because on Friday evenings after prayers, when the elders met in the square to eat, she was enlisted to pass the dishes, though she was not allowed to serve the men. The talk was of Babby. What to do with Babby. They argued fiercely.

One man spoke of a story, a true story he had read of girls returning from captivity only to plot the murder of their parents and their extended family. The mention of an orphanage was immediately shouted down, as all the orphanages were full. Camps were also full. Uncle wanted it to be disposed of at once. He was adamant. 'It has to go.' A neighbour asked him to show some compassion, saying that I had not gone willingly with my captors, inferring the torments I had endured and to remember that I carried an infant through all the dangers of the forest, when I could easily have left her to die.

Abigail saw how agitated I had become and had to pull me back from racing out of there at that very moment. She said nothing would be decided for weeks and weeks. There would be a big conclave of emirs and elders, many of whom would have to travel from different states, so that there was time, there was time.

Mama is calling to me to bring the sweet dishes. There are buns that we were given in the city, stale by now, but the icing still soft and sweet. There are also fruits, nicely peeled and wedged on a metal tray that we have been loaned – papaya, star apples, guava and passion fruit, arranged so that their colours complement each other. The guests are talking and laughing louder than they should. Everyone is very happy and I am ready to die.

Pastor Reuben came forward to welcome me home. He was in the same old smock that he always wore, claiming that the four pockets were useful to put things in. It had been stitched many times and patched in several places. He looked older, thinner and more shaken. His wife had since died, as he told me, and the church was gone, the church that everyone, including my father, had helped build. People travelled to bigger churches in the city and everything was more modern – microphones, loudspeakers, guitar music, pouring out into the yard outside, where the goats and their young nibbled on whatever they could find. The emphasis was less on scripture and more on soul-searching and entertainment. He looked into my eyes and saw the well of tears.

'I baptised you, Maryam,' he said out loud and to everyone's astonishment, placed his hand on my shoulder, guessing my distraughtness. He said that once a week there was a gathering in his house next to the church and women came from all over to share their stories and their burdens. I was always welcome.

Not too long after, the place emptied and I was alone with Mama and Uncle.

'Take broom,' Uncle said and I went back out into the yard and began to sweep up the debris and the burnt wood shavings.

I spoke to Babby. I did not know where Auntie's house was, but it was somewhere across those dark and sinister fields, across the black mud and the brown mud, across the hoardings and the burnt villages and oh my God, I would go there and I would find her.

*

I was out on the road the following morning and all the mornings waiting for her, the way my father had waited for me. I sat on the seat he had made. Sitting there I had a view of three roads and on one of those roads a car would be coming. I had been promised it.

People who passed by thought I was a little strange, talking to myself and singing the song that Buki and I sang when we walked in the forest.

Chumi, a friend of Mama's, came and sat beside me. She had a gift for me. I thought it a good omen. It was a coloured sewing book called *Projects Made Simple*. I would learn to sew. I would have a trade. Eventually, I might become a seamstress and build up a business. She was at pains to tell me of this new resurgence in sewing, due to a popular television programme. Sewing was no longer a pastime or a duty; it was mainstream. As she flicked through the pages, I saw coloured pictures of socks, slippers, tassels, pencil cases and a variety of bags. There were also detailed instructions on how to fit zip fasteners and shoulder pads.

Chumi was being so nice and friendly that I felt I could trust her. Could she help me to get my child back? Could she intercede with my mother and my uncle? In an instant she was up, flustered, enraged, her eyes fuming, saying what a sly and thankless girl I was. I must accept my fate, help my family and

I might find myself a husband and make more children. She fled so quickly that she forgot the sewing book. It was on my lap. I looked down at the cover, with its trellises of flowers and orange-chested birds.

*

Next morning, the letter was on the seat, held down with a stone. The paper was damp from dew. The outside read, *FROM A CLOSE RELATIVE WHO WISHES TO RE-MAIN ANONYMOUS.* The writing, which was in pencil, was in capitals, each letter separate from the next, as a decoy. In places the letters were blurred and then again in heavy black ink – *BABY JESUS COMMANDS YOU TO GIVE UP THIS CHILD.*

The earth is spinning. A whole hilltop has gone up into the sky. My eyes are bleeding. Flocks of lambs huddled together are being driven to their slaughter. They are bleating, bleating their last breaths.

Baby Jesus is plunging the knife.

UNCLE AND MAMA are setting out on a journey. They are dressed in their Sunday clothes. She will not say where.

I have the freedom to walk around and vent my rage. I talk to myself.

'Baby Jesus has taken Babby. Baby Jesus is cross with me. Mama is cross with me. Uncle is cross with me.'

I decide I will run away. I have no belongings. I know the road that leads to the market and passes the twisting yellowish river. Then, farm on all sides and soon after that, traffic, lots of traffic, the little tuk-tuk taxis, people hanging out of them, bringing chickens and corn and whatever they have to sell. The chickens screeching.

Once in the market I am safe. I can slip in and out between the crowds. I will eat rinds or anything that is thrown down. From there, I will make my way to where Rebeka is. Rebeka is not cross with me, but she has sickness.

I did not leave at once. I had scores to settle, walking around our kitchen, striking things.

There was an old bath out in the yard that was packed with sand. Big ugly weeds feeding on it. The sand was solid, first rain, then dry season, then rain and more dry season, on and on. A soiled brown colour. The weeds sulked at being flung down. I carried water from the well and met people on the way. I thought, when Mama and Uncle come back and miss me, these same people will tell them I hauled buckets of water. They won't find me.

As soon as the sand had loosened and was a bit flakier, I shovelled it onto the yard to make little dwellings.

Weirdly, words begin to pass through me. A blast of words, prayers and curses – 'Mother is so sweet, Mother is not so sweet.' My captors are speaking through me. Words and phrases that I did not know I knew, unless I heard them during lessons.

'*Sabo. Sabo. Sabo.*'

Blasphemy. Blasphemy. Blasphemy.

'*Raquki kuturwa*. I am a female leper.'

'My brother is gone to Kano. *Ya sam mini goro*. He got me a bit of kola nut.'

'*Ya ara min riga*. He lent me a sad grey gown.'

'Men overcame me in war . . . they took my money. They each had three wives . . . it is a sin that leads to death.'

Ba zan koma ba

Ka kama

Ki kama

Ku kama.

Seize. Seize. Seize.

Ku kai

Ku kama shi

Ki sa rana

I had not heard them, not even seen them, but my mother is frantic, calling, 'Nathan. Seize her, seize her,' as I try to run away. She is trembling with fear. She says the Jihadis have come and are going to kill us. I smile and give her a little friendly curtsy. *Allah ya rufa mana.* May God conceal our secrets.

Uncle has caught me. His hand on the nape of my neck, clutching it. He has also taken my phone, my last link to Pastor Reuben, or Abigail, or anybody.

I am being marched through the kitchen. Mama is petrified. Uncle puts black tarp on the window and she hands him little tacks to hold it down. They press it in at the corners. The room is pitch black. He stands above me, holding a mace. Two or three blows of that mace and my brain is pulp.

I am craven with them. I beg for mercy. I tell them I love them, which is not true, and that I will work on the farm. I will do anything rather than be locked up in this dungeon, because the Jihadis will find me and spirit me away.

*

The window is blocked up. The bars have been there a long time. Not a flicker of light shows through. At first I stood, thinking that someone might see my imprisoned shadow, but nobody does. I stand for hours, until it is so cold that I crawl back to bed and pull the cotton coverlet over my head, to vanish. In the deep silence, a wail was borne in from some dreaded lair.

Mama slept on a chair in the kitchen and at dawn, escorted me to the outside closet. The yard was a glaze of dew that I would have gladly lain on, but she hustled me along, not wanting anyone to see me. Later she left gruel on a plate outside the door. It was as if I was a leper.

So it went on, from dream to waking and back again. I cannot tell the difference, as I am inert. Later, I hear the apprehensions and sounds of night. Sometimes I am in the forest, an unfamiliar forest, emptied of all mankind. The trees are gigantic, their grey trunks gnarled. They are talking gnarled talk.

MAMA IS PULLING ME out of bed, dragging a comb through my hair, steadying me on my feet. We have visitors. Auntie and cousins have come to speak with me. They have news. I am led into the kitchen and see five women and a little girl with a brown cap, skulking in the corner. Her name is Pia. She is told to hand me things. She does it bashfully and avoids looking me in the eye. There is the green soother, with hanging wooden beads, a pair of knitted bootees and a dribbler. Auntie can barely speak with grief, her tears as plump as her pearls. Her nails are jet black, the pink of her cuticles so raw, and brazen.

'Babby is gone. Babby is no more.' It was a peaceful death, a cot death, which is not uncommon. How it broke their hearts, hers and Pia's.

They have come to share everything with me, every happy moment up to her last. Her bath each evening, which Pia called bubbles, and weighing her on the kitchen scales, so tiny was she. Her weight is inscribed in a little notebook, which Auntie feels as yet she is unable to part with. One day, she will let me read it and I will see how tenderly my child was cared for. All the time Pia is moving her head back and forth, like the shifting needle on the kitchen weighing scales. They have brought a cake. Mama suggests that everybody sit and have a piece of it. There are not enough chairs. The cake is three colours, yellow and brown and green. Funeral bread. They talk while they eat. The ice-cold certainty of her doom had not yet possessed me. Auntie dwells on the moment she heard Pia running down the hall, calling, 'Lady, lady, come quick,' and her going to the room and beholding this little dead effigy that was so recently a bonny treasure.

I hate them. I want to kill them.

I am whispering to Mama to please bring me to 'its' grave, I am already calling Babby 'it'. She hears what I am whispering and asks, telling them it is my one wish. They are sorry, but it is impossible. I must know that the baby had a proper burial according to ancient ritual and was dressed in a new white shroud. She had to be buried a long way from our region, in order to banish the lingering evil. The man who did it was a hired undertaker and had taken it to a border state, where its powers were nullified.

'Take me there,' I am shouting at them. I am telling them if their words mean anything, their hearts will thaw. There is a car outside that can fetch me. That is all I ask. I will accept her death if I am brought to her grave. They shake their heads. It cannot be. Auntie commences a prayer and the others join in.

In the midst of all that praying and breast-beating and hypocrisy, something inside me went black. I went towards it. I embraced it. I went inside it, into blackness.

FIRST IT WAS her shadow, then her ghost, the little figure in gossamer, her feet barely touching the ground.

'Babby,' I whispered. She did not answer. I was petrified.

After the third visit I was less afraid. It was always dusk when she came, while Mama was cooking something for Uncle. The glow from the gossamer of her dress shed light as a lamp would. She prowled. What did she want. She would not answer.

'I am lonely,' I tell her, and ask what is in store for me. Once I tried to touch her but she flittered from my grasp. Why does she always rummage. What is it she is looking for. Finally, I knew. With a glee she pulled it out. She dusts it off. It was the drawer lining I won for my essay on trees. I stare at it. 'Woods of Windsor'. How we cling to the merest fragment.

'Don't go, don't go,' I plead, but she has already gone leaving a strange perfume in the room, ethereal as an essence. Mama smells it when she comes in, sniffing around, saying, 'There's been someone here.'

She fears the Sect are going to come for me and is certain they have sent a siren to lure me away.

MAMA LAY ON THE BED beside me.

'What have I done . . . what have I done?' she keeps asking. We are better friends now. Again and again I ask her, implore her, can we go to the grave. She is constantly reproaching herself. Pastor Reuben is doing his best to get them to agree. Mama tells me that I talk in my sleep. I beg of her to bring us even to the cemetery gate, saying that if it is locked we can hold on to it and rattle it, we can yell through it and make ourselves heard.

'What have I done . . . what have I done,' she keeps saying it in daylight and in darkness.

'*O Lord, thou pluckest me out,*' I answer.

Uncle shouts from the kitchen that I should get up, that it is planting time and I should be in the farm.

'She is like a reed,' my mother answers.

I could not understand why I was telling her, but I was. I relive the day that I tried to drown Babby. With hunger, constant screaming and Buki dead, I had gone over the edge. I brought Mama with me on the walk, describing the long distances between the trees, a monkey that chased us from treetop to treetop and one bush with the shower of small pink flowers. Then the sight of the water itself, oval like a platter, so beautiful and silvery, and my lifting her down into the cool that she craved. I described the soft current swishing over her and she smiling a little smile of beatitude.

'Don't, don't,' Mama said. She could not bear to hear any more. She went out of the room, muttering to herself, her body stooped in atonement. Much later, she returned with things – a cassava fritter and a few raisins. I could not tell how she got them.

As time went on she became afraid that something was going to happen to me. She feared she might be up at the farm helping him and I would be all alone. She fetched a bell that had belonged to her ancestor who was a chieftain. It was a copper cowbell. I could alert a neighbour or a passer-by. The hammer had stalled from disuse, but I grasped it anyhow.

She would take me for short walks, to nurse me back to health, but everything, the people, the trees, the pump, were all shadows and I recoiled from my reflection in the puddles of water.

It was not too long afterwards and as a last resort, Mama decided to send for the witch woman.

THE WOMAN CAME in the dead of night. Her clothes were very colourful and she was carrying a bundle with all her medicines and plants and powders. She pulled out stalks, the earth still clinging to them, and told us she had gone to the most sacred part of the forest to find these remedies. Her feet were tired. She needed a drink of some kind. While Mama was gone, she kept sniffing and looked at me and said, 'Rapture . . . you are still enraptured.' I was too afraid to ask what she meant. Mama was then told to bring rags, a bowl of clean water and a fresh egg. For the second time, she was ordered out of the room.

I had to stand on the raw egg, first one foot, then the other, in order to be cleansed. Then she made me drink from a little beaker. The drink was the blood of a certain cow. She said the cow had not died, as the blood was taken from the vein with a special spear. They were men skilled at doing it. She was brusque, said she and her cohorts knew more than the psychiatrists and doctors in the land. Then she began chanting. I was supposed to follow her. She recited all the vowels and syllables of her clan to rout him out, to be rid of him.

We were walking in circles, clockwise, anticlockwise, until

finally I felt dizzy and swooned onto the bed. I began to cry. She took that to mean repentance. She was ready to heed spirit. Then she turned me on my back and I felt the sharp incisions, as with a razor she made slits to pack powders into the openings and press them down. I had to hold a wooden charm in my hand and earnestly ask to be let free of him, to let him go. I had no idea what she meant.

'The mother's milk is the child's curse,' she said and mine was no exception. While the child is connected to the father through blood, it is connected to the mother through milk and it was my cursed milk that caused my child to be taken from me in the first place. I had chosen him over her. It was why I also chose to end up in a darkened room with a black window, so that he could pass through whenever he wanted and dally with me in whatever way we wished. She was getting angry. She could see I was not responding, she could see that I was disobeying her, without the words. Her next implement was the needle. It was like a crochet needle, with a hook at its tip. She heated it on a tiny burner, testing until it sizzled, and then she thrust it down my throat, where she tore and tugged and shouted at him to be gone. Then weirdly triumphant, she brought up a bubble, the size of a small bead and almost luminous. She said we would see no more of him, the bubble was his seed and it was dissolving. He was gone. She had routed him. She called to my mother loudly. She needed sustenance, she needed milk.

'Will she be alright?' Mama asked, because she saw how intimidated I was.

'We have many gods who do as they decide,' was the perplexing answer.

There was the matter of payment. I knew we had no money.

They both went out and I guessed Mama paid her with a hen. I could hear the commotion in the yard, the hen squalling as its legs were being tied or maybe strangling her and the cockerel's wrath was mighty.

MAMA MARCHED IN like a warrior and strode across the room. Her face was gleaming wet and drops of rain perched on her hair. She had been to see Pastor Reuben. First thing, she tore the tarp off the window and it fell in soft clods onto the floor. Light at last. She was exhilarated. She kept murmuring as though to someone. She could not contain herself much longer. Finally, she bellowed it in my ear, first one ear and then the other – *That Baby is not dead, That Baby is not dead.* She had said it twice. It seemed impossible and yet it felt true. Why is this dust an infinity of rising glitter. Why is the moss on the tree outside no longer mouldy but a luminous green. Why is Mama not atoning. What does she know. How does she know. I got out of bed and for the first time walked without her help.

'How do you know,' I ask.

How does she know all this? She knows because Pastor Reuben has just told her. That is why he sent for her so early. He learnt it from a nun called Sister Angelina, who was visiting a sick relative nearby. Pia knew the nun and went to her in a great consternation, saying she would go straight to hell, as she had colluded in a crime. Although Auntie had promised to dispose of Babby and had been prepared to snuff her out, when the moment came, she did not have the stomach for it. Instead she hired a hoodlum who did all sorts of dirty work, putting down wild dogs, trapping rats, gathering firewood, priding himself on his skills as an entrepreneur. His name was Lucky. He even bragged that for the right money, he could bring the ex-President's head on a plate. Auntie met with him in secret. A few nights later Babby was taken in her sleep, bundled in her favourite wrapper that she had grown to love and was inseparable from.

Sister Angelina and Pastor Reuben were scheming to get her back. They knew Lucky would thwart them every second of the way. Sister was collecting money to buy him a cycle, even a second-hand cycle, as he was forever grumbling at having to traipse that forest daily. Even as Mama told me, floating on these billows of happiness, a shadow had come down. Over me. Over everything. We were wasting time. It was too late. Lucky would have sold her back to the Sect who would revel in it. Maybe they were already boasting of it on social media. I am back in that yard with all the men and machinery and Lucky carries Babby in and plonks her down. Little Norah runs towards her to try and pick her up in her arms, blood running down their thighs. Two bleeding sisters together, calling to their lost herds.

'Why are you shivering,' Mama asks.

I do not answer. Gone. Gone. The herd had fled to where the grass was sweeter, fled from bloodiness and scourge.

Dawa dawa dawa

Dawaaaaaaaaa

Waaaaaaaaaaaaaaa

Waaaaaaaa

Dawaaaaaaaaaaa

Dawaaaaaaaaaaaaaaaaaaaaaa

Dawaaaaaaaaaaaaaaaaaaaaaaaaa

Waaaaaaaaaaaaaa

Waaaaaaaaaaaaaaaaaaaaaaaaaaaaaaa

THERE WAS NO TRACK, just bushes and saplings falling into one another and coarse grasses taller than me. I had to wade through, but I was certain I had come to the right place, because of a yellowish light that puttered through the darkness. Sister Angelina had shown me a photograph of Lucky's ramshackle caravan, set down in a hollow. Even the slightest stir made me jump.

Sister Angelina had also told me that after the day's work in the forest, he came back to the caravan, smoked cannabis for relaxation and then had a short snooze. He grew the cannabis in pots at the side and claimed that it sharpened his wits.

I had to come and I had to come alone if ever I was to give myself the name of Mother.

Saying goodbye to my mother was unbearable. She knew I would not be returning. Her bony arms, her frail sinews, tightened around me and then she reached for Yusuf's shirt, pulled it from the wall, smelt it for the last time and bundled it into my grasp. She understood that Sister Angelina was taking me into hiding.

It was pitch dark suddenly and I kept tripping on mounds

and tree stumps, but my eyes remained fixed on that yellowish puttering light.

I knew from Sister Angelina that Lucky's daughter took Babby during the day, brought her back in the evening and put her in an outside shed, where she was given a bottle, which had to suffice until morning. I had not reckoned on that shed being locked. I searched for the key under stones and along the narrow ledge that skirted the blind side of the caravan, but it was not there. Through the wide slits in the wooden door I saw her, in a basket on the floor, holding something that seemed to be animal pelt. It was woeful, seeing her abandoned in her sad wandering world. What visions of desolation haunted her, what did she remember of us.

I went to look through the half-open shutter of the caravan, to make sure that Lucky was asleep. He was stretched out in his barber's chair, the one Sister Angelina had shown me a picture of, with silver arm rests and a rack for his feet. He was wearing only his underpants, with his sunglasses on the floor beside him. His body was scored with scars and gashes, as if he had just returned from battle. In contrast, he wore a lot of gold chains and various gaudy rings. There was a gun with a long grey nozzle, hanging on a bit of twine nearby. A kitchen drawer that had been pulled out was full of different kinds of knives and beside it, a wheel-shaped stone sharpener. There was something stewing on the top of a tiny little stove and new suits of clothing were on hangers, waiting to be resold. I had to be quick.

It took me merely seconds to go up those steps, push the door quietly in and search for the key. There was a bunch of keys of all sizes and metals, but the small shiny one, for a brand new padlock, was not among them. I crept. It was not in the drawer of knives, it was not on the window ledge and then, under a tray full of dirty dishes, I saw the glint of small keys tucked under a packet of powdered milk.

Out of habit, she clenched her little fists when I lifted her up, even though I had cuddled her and said her name repeatedly. She let out a cry that was both fiendish and frightened. Presently he was outside on the step and shouting the slaughter he would wreak on us. He knew my name. He knew where I lived.

I scuttled away in a different direction, towards nowhere, a sort of underworld. Not a chink of light came between the tall trees that were massed together. I held her to my chest. There were shots from different directions as he ran in search of us and after each explosion she quaked as if she was about to fall asunder, like the shedding pieces of a jigsaw. She did not know words, but she knew terror.

I held her tight, tighter, so as to scoop her up inside me, where she would be invisible to him. Him. Where was he now? The gun had gone silent. Perhaps he had run on ahead to apprehend us at some entrance. I had to keep reminding myself that I had come to rescue her and was driven on, clutching at whatever branch or bough I could find, to keep me upright. My feet had gone beyond pain and I walked, if there is such a thing as walking into eternity.

Then suddenly we are sliding down a fallen bough that has wedged itself into a choked ravine. Where are we? What has happened? The sound of my own voice and the chatter of running water is uncanny. Babby starts to bawl, sensing calamity. In that acreage of death I thought of spirits and how they must wander about both sensible and insensible to the pleas of the living.

'Buki,' I called. I felt her presence and then her absence, immediately followed by the absence of everyone I had ever known. Except we had to move, or otherwise Lucky would find us. On all fours I set out, Babby's face bobbing against mine, her hands thumping me with her hot temper. Perhaps she believed that I was bringing her back to the dungeon. But how would I ever know what she believed. I kept crawling and hushing her, until finally she lapsed into a jumpy sleep that can hardly have been a refuge, because every so often shudders of terror escaped her.

Gradually, there was a little light, as the overhanging branches were fewer and by a gap between some trees I saw a waiting moon. There was the trundle of a vehicle and then another and I reckoned we could not be that far from some road or other. Then under some bushes a silhouette appeared, that seemed to be a woman's. It was Sister Angelina running towards us, disbelieving and agitated.

'Why did you do such a crazy thing?'

'We have her,' I said.

'Crazy,' she repeated and walked on muttering, and I followed her to where her car was hidden under a copse. The moment we got in she turned on the radio full blast. It was to stop quarrelling. The music was the loudest and most jangling I had ever heard. She drove recklessly and in defiance of all rules. Other cars hooted and one driver stuck his head out the window and told her to get back in the bush where she belonged.

It was only when we got to Pastor Reuben's house that I saw how distraught she had been. She drew up her sleeves, raised her bare arms, eschewing all niceness, all piety, haranguing the saints to whom she ceaselessly prayed.

'It was out of love . . . pure love,' Pastor Reuben said quietly.

'And pure madness,' Sister Angelina countered, as she went into the little disused sacristy and we could hear her retching.

The room had been stripped of furniture. There was a long bench and some wicker cribs, for mothers to lay their infants into, during their weekly sessions. Along the top of a small bookcase was a series of jagged waxen roses and inside, sheathed in cobweb, were papers and pamphlets. He was doing everything to be hospitable, coaxing Babby to sup from a mug that he held for her. Almost immediately after, she fell into a profound sleep.

Sister came and sat near me on the bench, tears running down her cheeks and contrite now. We sat in silence knowing that the door might be burst open at any point.

It was very early next morning when we left Pastor Reuben's house, so as not to be sighted.

He stood on the step, proud and erect, as happy as if it was his own life that had been spared.

'Don't forget us,' he said. It seemed more like an exchange between living and dead, as though his ghosthood was already on him.

AS THE DOUBLE DOORS of the convent were opened for Sister Angelina to drive in, I smelt blossom. Blossom everywhere, even draping the low building itself. Flower-beds surrounded the low stools of box hedging. The sun is shining.

Just inside the small reception hall nuns are waiting to welcome us and still others are running from different directions, their veils fluttering as they hurry. Each one shakes hands with me. They embrace Sister Angelina. They can't stay. They have duties. They teach catechism. *Catechists*, they are called. They have badges on their blouses that say so. There is a smell of wax polish. From a stained-glass window high above sunlight is pouring in and on the floor a mosaic of marvelling blues. There is a wooden altar with a statue of St Francis, who is the patron saint of their order, and around it on the ledge there are several petitions.

When I see Sister Angelina put on her brown knitted cap again, I know that she is leaving. She has to return to the little school where she and another nun share the teaching. The car that brought us there is waiting to take her to the bus station and the journey will be over five or six hours.

'So many poor people . . . so many children,' is all she says. She will write to me.

Babby and I are alone with Sister Christiana, who leads us into the dining room, saying we must be tired and we must be thirsty. Everything so calm, so orderly. The walls are a pale yellow and there are small round tables covered in crimson patterned cloths, which are obviously the tables where the nuns eat, with little sprays of dried flowers in tiny bottles on each one. The muslin curtains along the bay windows obscure the big high wall beyond.

Babby has fallen asleep. Sister brings a glass of water for me. It is ice cold. It is from one of their cold wells. They are lucky, she says, as they have three wells in all and moreover, clean brooks that run down from the plateau. The water from those brooks is so special it even removes the stains from their white blouses. It is where they bathe and where they also wash their blouses. She sees that I am forlorn and brings me a book as a gift. It is the first book I have ever owned. There is a picture of Christ on the cover, holding a staff and embracing a lamb which has a crescent of blood on the ridge of its back. It is a book of daily reflections. I open it at the prayer for that day and read:

In the days when the judges ruled there was a famine in the land, and a certain man of Bethlehem in Judah went to sojourn in the country of Moab, he and his wife Naomi and his two sons. But Elimelech, the husband of Naomi, died, and she was left with her two sons. These took Moabite wives; the name of the one was Orpah and the name of the other Ruth. They lived there about ten years; and both sons died, so that the woman was bereft of her two sons and her husband. Then she started with her daughters-in-law to return from the country of Moab, for she had heard in the country of Moab that the Lord had visited his people and given them food. And Orpah kissed her mother-in-law and went back, but Ruth clung to her. And she said, 'See, your sister-in-law has gone back to her people and to her gods; return after your sister-in-law.' But Ruth said, 'Entreat me not to leave you or to return from following you; for where you go I will go, and where you lodge I will lodge; your people shall be my people, and your God my God.' So Naomi returned and Ruth the Moabitess her daughter-in-law with her, who returned from the country of Moab. And they came to Bethlehem at the beginning of barley harvest.

*

The young nun who cooks has brought a white plastic chair for me into the garden. She wants me to eat more. At lunch she poured an extra amount of the meat gravy on the rice she had put down before me. As a special treat there were pancakes afterwards, pancakes with maple syrup.

Babby wants to play. The little pathway to the entrance door is made up of pebbles and she is intrigued by them. She picks them up, staggers a few steps and then throws them down. She goes back to pick up more and flops in the rompers that they have got for her. She takes her time before deciding to cry or to get up. She gets up and gathers two more fistfuls of pebbles, which trickle through her fingers and make her laugh. It is an almost unnatural laugh, the first real laugh in her life.

A man has come to do the garden. With a hoe he is taking all the weeds between the paving stones and throwing them onto a heap. There is a little boy with him. The boy is curious about us. The father has thrown down a long weed and Babby decides that it will be hers, so that she can thwack things. The boy wants it. She won't give it back. They tussle. The weed breaks and the boy bites her with rage. It is more a nip than a bite. She is yelling, pointing to the spot where his teeth bit. It is not bleeding, but she is making the most of it. The little boy is sent back to his house, a tiny house, which is just beyond the rectangle of hedging. He looks back hating us. I say to the father that I am sorry. I should not have been so absent-minded. He tells me not to worry and asks if I have ventured out. He opens one half of the double doors. I see a world of men, so many men, on cycles, driving goats, carrying goods on their head, all of them busy with some chore or other and taking no notice of me. Yes, I am afraid of them. I am afraid of what they might do to me. I am afraid to go beyond the confines of that high wall.

*

In the evening, we are brought to our quarters. It is a little house on the far side and as we cross the courtyard I see cats hiding under the two motorcars and a truck, nuzzling down for the night. The two cars, a sister tells me, are for taking nuns to the hospital or meeting visitors at the bus station. The reason why we could not occupy the room earlier is that a bishop had been staying for a week. He comes regularly for the peace and quiet. Also nuns come from their different houses all over the world. In the dining room, I had heard them talk of a nun who was shortly to come from Ireland. Her name is Sister Rosario and they are making a shawl for her, with many roses stitched into it, to match her name. Three nuns worked at it from different sides of the tapestry. They sing her praises. She is old. They wonder if she will like the shawl, or if perhaps she will think it a little too gaudy. They also wonder if she will wear it over her shoulders or over her knees when she sits in her rocking chair, saying her rosaries. What they do not say is when she is coming.

Our dwelling is small and everything has been readied and cleaned. There is a jug of water and a baby's bottle with two clean teats. Sister leads me into the reception room, which itself leads to the bedroom, with a thin, gold-coloured curtain to draw across. She tells me that the dogs will come out in a short while, so that I must not cross the yard again until morning. Having no guns or men to protect them, the dogs are their only safeguard.

Then we are left alone.

Babby does not want to get ready for bed. She wants to play. This time it is with the curtain. By tugging at it she realises she can draw it. She goes behind it, hides and then peeps out and goes 'Boo'. The next game is to pull on the curtain and decide as to whether she or it is the stronger. I have to be sure that she doesn't pull too hard, or it will be taken off its hooks and we will be in trouble.

I have to coax her to have a bath. Once in it she is pleased. They have placed a littler bath in the big bath and there is a duck for her as a new friend. She loves the towels and the face towels. They are yellow, with the word *Visitor* stitched in black at the corner. She also loves the soap that the nuns themselves make. It is the colour of butterscotch and I have to stop her from putting it in her mouth, because she assumes it is sweet. Once in the bath, she is distracted and determined to wreak small punishment on her new duck.

It is dark when the dogs are let out. They howl and howl, excited at being freed. I cannot see them. I dare not pull the curtain aside, or they will leap up. I get into bed.

*

I waken each night in that room thinking, *Where will we go.* My dreams are bizarre. Sometimes I am on a journey with other mothers and children and then turfed out of the truck in a lonely bit of countryside, in batches. The driver bids us a merry goodbye, glad to be rid of us.

When the dogs are brought in at dawn, I stand by the window and see the last of the moon, breathlessly beautiful, with a halo around it.

THERE WERE NO GATES. We just walked into a huge courtyard swarming with people, children marauding around and one melancholy goat, tethered to a post, bleating away.

Two dogs, all bone, ran around, barking hysterically at one another. The steward who was showing us around said that people bought these animals to try and fatten them up and then resell them at a profit. Everyone, as he said, trying to scrape a livelihood.

Word had been sent to the convent that a room should become vacant, and Sister Christiana hated breaking the news to me. Even as we were leaving the little guesthouse, fresh flowers were being put in a vase and holy water sprinkled on them, to welcome Sister Rosario. Sister Christiana gave me farewell gifts – chapatis, cereal and a pot of guava jelly. Then she took a medal from her vest, pinned it to my collar and made the sign of the cross on my forehead. It was in veneration to the tongue of St Anthony.

The camp had been a school at one time and now housed hundreds of displaced people. It was a two-storey structure that occupied three sides of a square with the courtyard in between. There was an air of improvisation. Women were queuing to get water, others bickering for their place in the queue by one of the three fires, and still others trying to wash their children from pitchers of water or the one leaking hose.

Our room was on the ground floor. A cotton curtain divided it from the noisy corridor. People passed back and forth all the time. There was a mattress, a thin sheet and in the corner a little brazier with pieces of crushed charcoal.

We put our belongings down as the steward was eager for us to continue the tour and get our bearings. He pointed to the latrines, and whispered to me that at night it was more usual for women to go in batches of three or four. Outside, on the opposite wall, was a derelict shed with the word *Medical* in large print. The door was locked. It had been long since abandoned. Further along there was a prayer room and I asked the steward if I might go inside. It was tiny with an adjoining vestry, vestments on a table and a tin bowl for holy water. A consecration bell lay sideways on a saucer, it tinkled eerily as we walked past it. There was a picture of Christ in scarlet, with an inscription, *O God is forever and ever*. The steward explained that the chapel opened for services some Sundays, but pastors could not come regularly as they had to serve the numerous camps all around.

Outside, young men sat on the ground, playing some kind of card game. Children were playing in their designated corner. It was a game in which they jumped from one small square of clay to another, avoiding the dividing lines, and the winner was rewarded with a speckled marble, which they all coveted.

Nearby, an oldish man beckoned to me to come and sit by him. He had a little food in a plastic bag and though he did not touch it, from time to time he looked in at it to make sure it was there. His name was Daran, which meant 'Born at night'. Babby tottered about but the other children scorned her because she was too young and meddlesome, wobbling in and out between the squares and interrupting their game.

'I will not die in this camp,' Daran said, thankful to have someone to listen to his story at last.

I will die a free man. My house is still standing. A woman told me so. The house I built with my own hands. Three years it took. I had three bedrooms with a water hole nearby so that I was able to build a bathroom. The tiles of the roof are a milk white so that it can be seen from far off. I left everything behind. I ran for my life. My wife was not there. I have not heard word of her since. I do not know where my children went, maybe with her, maybe not. My house is all I have left. The Jas Boys vandalised and burnt all the other houses, but not mine, because of its three bedrooms and also a yard where they could do drills. They had three rooms to sleep in. I learnt all this from a woman called Fatima, who peddled from place to place. She too lived under the Mandara mountains. She came by here one day, selling soup. A yellow soup that she made from mustard seed and packed in small plastic pouches. She recognised me. She told me that my house was still standing. She and her husband had been taken together, but she would not convert whereas her husband did. He asked her not to fight with them, to make life easier for both of them. She refused. He is dead now, or so she thinks. She has no love left for him. She stole a bicycle and escaped her village, she lived in a cave that was also the site of a mass grave, and as a result overcame her fear of death. Eventually, she started up a small business selling soups, because she always had a knack for cooking. I met her by chance. I was begging a farmer up yonder for a tiny bit of land to grow maize – 'If you don't work, you don't eat.' He had a hard heart. I kept going back, doing little things for nothing, clipping hedges and so forth. One of his children got sick in the mind, and his wife told him, 'Give Daran a perch of land and God will repay us.'

He took five short steps, put pegs down, and said, 'This is your ground for the next six months.' It is all I have. With the little money I have accrued I will leave here, I will make my way to the Mandara mountains and fill my eyes with the vision of my white roof. If it is occupied I will go to the military. I will show them my papers. I will be reinstated.

'Arise, O compatriots,' he said, as he stood, his arms outstretched, his eyes full of a crazed certainty.

The children, who had heard the story many times, threw clods of clay at him.

*

The classroom was long since abandoned. It was where people charged their phones and from the two wall sockets, a huddle of different coloured phones. Cable wires branched and looped together. Sitting there opposite a blackboard, I thought I could hear the voices of the young children who had been in this very classroom and sat on those very benches. It was an unfinished English lesson. The teacher had written the letters 'Si' on the blackboard, and under it were a list of words that she had encouraged the children to find for themselves:

Silk
Sift
Sim card
Sip
Sir
Sit
Sieve
Sigh
Sight

Then a big woman came in, talking to herself. Her sleeves were rolled up, either because she had just been in a fight or was intending to. She looked at me as if I should not be there. Then she went to the jumble of phones, searched for her own, picked it up, put it to her ear, listened, and said, 'Bastard.'

'That woman has mental problems,' she said, as she sat on the floor, with a child between her legs, totally mute.

'That woman has mental problems.' She gloated at the harm she would do to her before the night was out and recited her various afflictions:

My husband and I were happy in the tailoring business. We made suits for weddings. He did the measuring and the cutting and I did the sewing. Business slackened a bit after the oil boom crashed, as grooms could not afford the bridal jewellery and the brides' parents were mortified at not being able to buy furniture for the new home. Nevertheless, we didn't fold. Then one evening, as I was carrying two new suits across the fields, for a groom and his best man, the Jas Boys caught up with me on their cycles.

'How are you,' they said, pleased to relieve me of the suits of clothing, and before I could escape, I was already theirs, my wrists tied with chains. We rode for hours and when we came to a mountain cave they stopped for the night. They took turns raping me. I was brought to one of the camps and put to work sewing and stitching for the wives. Soon I was pregnant. I only escaped because the wife of one commander, who was besotted with him, sent me to the village to choose the nicest underwear. In that village I met a lorry driver with whom I did business in exchange for a ride a few kilometres from my own village. The sign that read 'Tailoring' was gone. I knocked on the door and a woman answered. Your husband don't love you, she said to

me. She said it several times. He did not like being spoken for. He came forward saying that we must live together, it was a condition of our religion and we would have to share. That was only the start of it. She still did the cooking. She still slept with him. We quarrel. We all end up here. He lost his business, he lost himself, disappearing for days.

A phone rings, and she springs like a panther to get to it – 'Where are you. How did it go. When are you coming back,' and then I hear her listening, and knowing she is about to be cut off she shouts into the phone, 'I love you.' She came back, retrieved the baby where she had left it and where it seemed to lapse back into a kind of coma.

'What did he say when you said "I love you"?' I asked.

'He said, "I know,"' and then she looked around, forlornly.

Three days previous he had set out on the long walk to the city. Someone had seen a sign on a window, *Tailor Wanted*, and he decided he would go there, find a job and get a separate house for each family. But even as she said it, she knew he had absconded.

*

A few lit cigarettes flicked through the darkness. I thought I was dreaming, until I wakened and heard people coming through the open gateway, still others creeping out from their holes and corners, to do business. It was the hour of buying and selling and bartering. Men had come to sell food, medicines or whatever they had. Older people came out to plead, to implore. One woman almost knelt. She asked for one pill, just for that one night, so that she could sleep. One night's blankness. She would pay when she could. A man swore at her and she shuffled off. Human nature on bended knee. Girls came to sell their favours, in order to get food for themselves and their children. Some had men pushing them forward, as they bargained and taunted the dealers. There were scuffles. *Don't touch her, don't touch her.* Two opposing cliques fought over a particular girl, the known beauty. The security guard was off duty and moreover, would be helpless with this crew. Everything was quick and furtive. An older man intervened and those who had a few naira bought what they could and withdrew to their rooms. Younger couples hurried towards the small alcoves by the church and behind the school, while still others went through the open gateway, out into the cleaner fields.

It wakened Babby. It frightened her. She clung to me, her feet kicking my stomach. I tell her she is safe. *We are safe.* I promise her the thing she loves. Semolina. Semolina. She knows the word by heart. I had got the brazier fitted up and with the little money I earned from doing farm work, I was able to buy things. She watched as I stirred and stirred the semolina, pressing the lumps with a wooden spoon, bruising them against the side of the saucepan. She was hawing in anticipation. We ate sitting on the floor and then licking whatever was left on our fingers.

We were safe. I had put a magic boundary between us and all that lay beyond. The cotton curtain was our fortification.

ONCE A MONTH BABBY and I went back to the convent. We set out very early when it was still cool and I resumed my old habit of counting the thousand steps at a time, as I had done with Buki. The welcome was gleeful. Two folded pancakes with maple syrup poured over them awaiting us. Babby recognised her surroundings, ran around scraping the metal chasing on the front of a settee, which had always fascinated her. Then she found the cream lace antimacassar, which she put on her head to look clownish. They had a surprise for me. Who should tell me? The honour was given to Sister Christiana. It was a letter propped by the little vase of flowers in the centre of the table. I read it quickly, and thought I might be hallucinating.

My dear friend, Sister Angelina wrote,

   I have good news. Masses were said. We have found a post for you. Poor Mother Pius went back to Verona on holiday and had a fall. Her health was declining and she had been so brave. Well into her eighties, but too stoic to let any of us know. We need a second teacher, as I cannot do it all alone. They are rascals, as I think I told you. I have been given permission from the Mother of my Order.

The children are also looking forward to your arrival and I think they are a little disappointed that they do not yet have uniforms, to show off when you arrive. A rich lady in Lagos has sent word that she is going to contribute towards our school and towards their educational programme. She learnt about us on the internet. How kind the world can be at times.

But let me not digress. You will find our village here in the plateau, printed in small lettering on the convent map. One of the sisters will bring you to the taxi station. It costs 1,200 naira and babies can travel for free. The driver, if he is friendly, will take you and will ask other colleagues in the taxi to contribute even a little money. Tell him that you are coming to teach and he will be pleased. There are rivers along the way where you might want to get out, but the driver cannot stop, as there is no time. He has to make two journeys per day and it is a long way from Jos. Bring a bottle of water and nappies for the baby. The drive is long and quite jolting. You will come off the main road and onto a still rougher road, with stones flying up in all directions. He will drop you in our village, which comprises six houses in one compound and a big baobab tree where people rest. You will be hot and hungry. If you knock on any door and say, 'Please can I have a drink for my baby,' they will give you milk or water, or whatever they have. They will give you food if they have it. No one will turn you away. Rest awhile and then carry on. Children will point the way. It is a steep walk up the hill to our little *structure, which is brown, with a zinc roof, also stained brown from the rain.*

*

She met me long before the hilltop, she ran down, brimming with excitement and put Babby on her back. First thing she gave us was a local drink made from millet, saying it would sustain us until we had supper. Proudly she pointed to the garden, and the neatly tended furrows, with beans, garlic, cassava and peanuts. Their two goats had rambled off, but she was certain they would return, as they liked their little shelter. She pointed to me to go alone to the prayer room, where I could give thanks to God. It too was small. There was a wooden dais, with a big Bible opened at a certain page. A crucifix hung from the wall, a gold crucifix with a raised ruby heart. I guessed that it was a gift from the bishop, because earlier she had told me how lucky they were with donations they had received. The governor gave them land to build a house and make a garden and Bishop James called on various government sources and held a grand reception in his villa for the inauguration.

The classroom, which also served as the dining room, was crammed with chairs stacked together, books on the table, a blackboard and various things the children had forgotten. Babby was tottering around, getting to know her new surroundings, finding things, a stick daubed with clay and a knitted doll. She liked the doll and began to kiss it and then have fights with it. It was sweltering. Pointing to pallet beds, Sister Angelina said the nuns sometimes slept there. A local man had made them, in exchange for the loan of their donkey, which he needed to fetch building materials between two small farms, as he was making a second house for his second family. She said the fathers tended to take more than one wife and that led to more children and lingering disagreements. In some instances, the mothers did not like the first children and there were squabbles as to who ate what, who sat at the table and who slept in the husband's bed on different nights. Eventually, the first family, or even the second family, were made to leave, some going to cousins and some to run away. The children grew up fast, they had to.

We ate at the classroom table, where she had put a cloth at one end. It was a white cloth, embossed with red silk rosebuds. Hundreds, if not thousands, of stars rested on a baize of the heavens.

She had gone to great lengths with the cooking. Our first course was parsley in a tasty soup. The seeds she had brought from the Mother house planted randomly, and yet they had taken. 'If you don't grow parsley, you'll never get your man,' she said, mischievously. I asked if she had been in love before she became a nun and the question slightly unsettled her. She took time to consider her answer. Yes. She had been in love. He was an older man, who held a very strong appeal for her, except that he was married. Unlike many others, he would not take a second wife and suggested that she might marry his brother. But that was not what she wished. It was, as she put it, a brief temptation from her true path.

After the soup, we had a different corn dish, a maize which she had ground overnight and then put through a sieve and flavoured with sweet chillies. There were also ground peanuts. Knowing we would feel thirsty, she had made a drink from goat's milk. The taste of it filled me with a remembered sweetness of my time with my Fulani Madara. In my wishful thinking, I hoped that she and my mother would meet some day on the altar of peace.

As the evening went on, Sister got more talkative. It was when she started to tell about her children, her little clan that walked two or three kilometres every day to the school, she became elated. They had become her life. The difficult thing of course was to try and discipline them. On any excuse their minds wandered and yes, they could be hot-tempered, they could be testy. When there were not enough pencils to go around, what she had to do was halve the pencils with a razor blade. Some brought their lunch, which was porridge in a plastic bag, carried around their necks like trophies. Others had no lunch, because their parents had nothing to give them. They held back, or hid under the chairs, sobbing with shame. She said it was touching to see how everyone wanted to share. What she and Mother Pius did was to put all the porridge in the big pot, add more boiling water and make enough gruel to go around. The children ate quickly. Then they were made to take a short rest, which they resented, being eager to get to the dancing. The beat of the music was in their bones and in their blood and it was funny to see them dance so freely like little men, their hips sashaying, their torsos rippling like waves, the boys acting as chaperons, staring up at the girls. Although they held hands they never kissed, kisses were for mama. After that they would not settle again, ran around chasing butter-flies or grasshoppers, boasting about the number of ants they swallowed and having battles. She had to keep them occupied until it was time to line them up in twos and threes and send them down the long road, to their scattered huts.

She had saved it for the end, like the good wine in the gos-pels. It was a rolled-up cache of drawings. Mother Pius had encouraged the children to paint some aspect of their lives, their houses, their parents, their brothers and sisters and their country. Some had done scrawls and squiggles that were mean-ingless, but the prize pieces she kept until last. There were three in all. A triptych.

The first was a panel of red, hard and obstinate slabs, with ochre vergings of blood dripping off the edges of the paper. It was called *War*.

The second was a drab grey, with a crush of children's faces staring out of a window, in a sustained and silent scream. It was called *Home*.

The third was a leafy green vista, full of growing things – maize, corn, rye and sorghum, all ripening together. The effect was lifelike, as if a cool breeze had made those leaves quiver, as it would before a shower of rain. It was called *Harvest*. Then she folded them carefully and held them to her person with a fervour.

It was time for bed. The stars, as she said, were turning in and so should we, as the children liked to set out very early in the morning.

*

I could not sleep. The tarpaulin on the roof of the bedroom had been rolled back. The stars had all gone in and the sky was gold, a dome of gold from end to end, its lustre so bright that it seemed as if the world was on the edge of a new creation. We were safe. We had found a home, at least for now. I was filled with an ecstasy such as I had never known. Spools of light filled the room and lit up the universe outside. All was stillness. In that moment of unalloyed hope and happiness, it seemed to me that those rays were pouring into the darkest dimensions of the land itself.

ACKNOWLEDGEMENTS

IMMEASURABLE THANKS TO the great number of people who helped me over the three years of writing this novel. Firstly my publishers, the great Faber & Faber, and in particular my occult editor Lee Brackstone, along with the two beacons, Rachel Alexander and Kate Burton, who had the crucial task of steering it through various media avenues. The renowned Jonathan Galassi, friend and editor of Farrar, Straus and Giroux, was my champion on the far side of the Atlantic.

My consummate agent Caroline Michel and her assiduous team worked indefatigably to have the book published in several countries.

Aosdana generously helped with travel towards my first journey to Nigeria.

Before leaving England, I made a few contacts. First and foremost, the enlightening Teju Cole, and Sven Hughes, who wisely warned me of the pitfalls ahead. Then the authors Elnathan John and Andrew Walker, who led me to Gerhard Müller-Kosack, who had lived in the Gwoza Hills for many years and was the keeper of the oral language of the local people, now alas vanished. Funmi Iyanda wrote a letter of introduction to Dr Oby Ezekwesili, who conceived the brilliant slogan 'Bring Back Our Girls'. Sam Taylor of Médecins Sans Frontières led me to invaluable sources.

Arriving in Abuja, the capital, at pre-dawn, I was met by the Irish ambassador Seán Hoy, who, with his wife Susan, welcomed me to the embassy. Seán's assistant, Dorothy Barraquias, helped me each morning, bringing the newspapers, all in English, and endeavouring to contact a great number of people and organisations. Soon, I am trying to get my bearings among the crowds, with its hungers, its markets, its debris, and yes, its great vitality, but what I wanted was to meet girls who had been taken by Boko Haram. With the help of Dr Oby, and her assistant Deborah Olumolu, I would meet Rebecca, Abigail, Hope, Patience, Fatime, Amina, Hadya, and many others, all with stories to tell but constrained by their reserve and delicacy. Most of them had babies who were spotlessly clean and wrapped in white shawls. Subsequently, I met doctors, psychiatrists, trauma specialists, NGOs and voluntary workers from all corners of the world. The journalist Ahmad Salkida gave me an insight into Boko Haram machinations and their bargaining skills. Kim Toogood brought my attention to the plight and sometimes ostracising of girls who had been captured and were labelled, even by their own clan, as 'Bush Wives'. I visited various IDP camps, met hoards of children and needing mothers, but very few men. Father David showed me around my first camp, which opened my eyes to the destiny of women with nowhere to go. Many followed me down the track and my interpreter, John Dghwede, said they were pleading with us to rescue them.

From Abuja, I travelled to Jos, which was a long drive and sometimes unnerving. I was welcomed by the Franciscan Sisters to a guest house where normally visiting priests or bishops came to a retreat. Sister Christiana and Sister Nora saw to my needs and I had happy conversations with a very young sister, Rita Satum, whose tiny convent was at the far end of the Plateau State. I also met Sister Antoinette and Sister Anne, both Irish. The anthropologist Adam Higazi, with his cousin Yusuf Habu Na'ango, brought me to the Kaduna State, where we visited two Fulani camps, or *wuro*, as they are named. That landscape and their way of life differed so radically from the teeming masses. Much as I loved my convent quarters, their dogs, their only guards, barked ferociously all night. Once again I was on the move, and, through the influence of Seán Hoy, I stayed in a compound with a garrulous and marvellous Irishman, Timothy McPeake, who with his team were responsible for the building and upkeep of the roads. Timothy whetted my interest in the myriad aspects of the country – rich and poor, thriving and woebegone, a modern Babel with a legion of stories.

While in Jos I visited Women for Women International, where Antonia Olieh and Bukola Onyishi had organised a group of women who had all suffered deprivations of a different kind. Their fears were of their farms being raided by Fulani herdsmen, and some spoke of husbands or sons who did not come back from their farms, and whose remains they had to search for. At the end I was presented with the brightly coloured honorary robe, in which, to my embarrassment, I was photographed.

The list grows, and includes Anna Badkhen, Sendi Dauda, Fatuma Hamidali Ibrahim, Fatima Akilu, and Dr Peter Ebeh, whose insight into the secret history of the captured girls was devastating. It was then I decided that my only method was to give the imaginative voicings of many through one particular visionary girl.

There were friends back in Europe, Dr Evelyn Stern, Jonathan Ledgard, and once again, the indefatigable Sven Hughes. Clodagh Beresford and Carlo Gebler (for a sudden epiphany), Richard and Ajjua Rickson (proposed taking me to some dancing in a church), Sasha Gebler (provided essential plot improvement) and friendly worshipers in Nigerian Churches and Houses of Praise scattered throughout London also had stories and happier memories to relate.

Last but not least, the workers, that diligent, ever-obliging succession of people who typed it again and again, starting with my stalwart of twenty-five years, Nadia Proudian, and in her absence, Louise Hardy, Rebecca Wearmouth, Amber Medland, Anna Martin, and ultimately, Sally Hayden, a young and brilliant journalist, whose research was so exigent and whose availability extended to the midnight hours.

I would finally like to thank Kate Ward of Faber, who oversaw the uneasy emergence of the manuscript, and Lucy Irvine from Caroline's team, for enduring frenzied last-minute corrections, until the time had come to let it Go.